'What about men?' Alec asked

Christine studied his expression, then sighed and gave up. 'Jeffrey Thurbern about four years ago. And last year there was...' She struggled trying to remember. 'Bruce Davidson.'

Alec wrote that down, then looked expectantly at her. 'Go on.'

Christine shook her head.

'Are you telling me that you haven't been with a man for over a year? Is there some problem?'

His gaze searched her face, his expression that of quizzical astonishment, and then he slid an arm around her waist and pulled her to him. 'I'll find out for myself.'

Christine was stunned by a multitude of sensations. His hand against her back so warm she could feel his fingers through her thin silk blouse. His scent filling her nostrils. His breath against her face. His body pressing hard against her own.

She made a small sound that was half objection, half appreciation. He slid his tongue across her bottom lip, then stroked it into her mouth, while the hand on her back caressed lower, urging her hips forward. It felt erotic and wicked and sinful and...absolutely wonderful.

Finally the kiss ended and he smiled. 'I'm pleased to report that there isn't

For my dad, Archie
and my brother and pal, Brian
love you lots, guys

'Writing a romance novel can be as exhilarating as a moonlight gallop, as exciting as a passionate kiss and, sometimes, as painful as a root canal. But it's never boring,' says **Alyssa Dean**.

That's why she writes romance. Alyssa finds something wildly exciting about bringing imaginary people to life, putting them in an almost impossible situation, and trying desperately to think their way out of it. Her characters become so real to her that they seem like actual people, and when they finally ride off together into the sunset, she feels as if her best friends have left forever. But then Alyssa begins again, bringing new characters to life, dreaming up another adventure, and starting a new romance.

ALYSSA DEAN is also the author of these novels in *Temptation*®:

MAD ABOUT YOU
THE LAST HERO

RESCUING
CHRISTINE

BY

ALYSSA DEAN

MILLS & BOON®

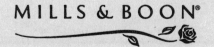

*MILLS & BOON and MILLS & BOON with the Rose Device
are registered trademarks of the publisher.
TEMPTATION is a registered trademark of
Harlequin Enterprises Limited, used under licence.*

*First published in Great Britain 1998
by Harlequin Mills & Boon Limited,
Eton House, 18-24 Paradise Road, Richmond, Surrey TW9 1SR*

© Patsy McNish 1997

ISBN 0 263 81082 8

21-9805

*Printed and bound in Great Britain
by Caledonian International Book Manufacturing Ltd, Glasgow*

1

IF THAT GUY was a paid assassin, he wasn't getting rich doing it.

Christine held the living-room curtains aside a cautious inch and peered through the rain-spattered windowpane. The front of the cottage property was a green mass of wild grass and trees, with a narrow driveway at the side leading to the back. That driveway was now occupied by an ancient, rusting blue sports car Christine had never seen before.

She didn't recognize the sandy-haired man who'd just emerged from it, either. He was medium height, dressed in wrinkled tan pants, a black, untucked T-shirt and a brown blazer—all of which looked like they'd been acquired at a thrift shop. The distance between them, the drizzling rain and his unnecessary sunglasses made it impossible to clearly see his features. However, he seemed more dishevelled than sinister. Unless he worked for Rent-a-Loser Hit Man Agency, there was a strong possibility that he was harmless.

Then again, maybe that harmless, dishevelled look was a standard hit-man disguise.

"Oh, for goodness sake," Christine exclaimed. She let the curtain drop and took a quick step backward. There was no reason to suspect the man out there had a sinister purpose.

Except for the twitch in her left thumb.

Christine tucked the thumb under the other fingers of her left hand and held it steady. According to her friend, that twitch was nothing more than a sign she'd been working too hard. Estelle believed Christine's uneasiness was the result of a "slight case of paranoia."

She took another peek out the window. Because of the angle, she could no longer see the man. She could hear him, though, climbing the stairs to the front porch. There was silence, followed by the squeak of the top step, then the hollow sound of knuckles striking the wooden door.

Christine took a step toward it, then stopped. Maybe she *was* being paranoid. On the other hand, there was no reason for a stranger to be here. The Calypso Canyon ski resort was probably a hub of activity during the winter. However, in the middle of August, it was more like a ghost town. It was remotely located, half an hour outside of Banff, Alberta. The road to it didn't lead anywhere else, and there wasn't anything to do here in the summer. The lodge at the base of the ski hill was closed, as was the attached convenience store. There were a few private cottages like this one around, but not many were occupied.

Christine hadn't seen much of the other people staying here, but she had seen cars—and none of them were decrepit, rusty blue sports cars.

Therefore, this man wasn't a neighbor, dropping by to borrow a cup of sugar. She didn't think he could be a friend of her brother, Keith, who owned this cottage. Keith was spending the summer in Europe. Surely all his friends knew that.

"You *are* acting paranoid," she scolded herself. The man could have a simple reason for his visit. Perhaps he'd stopped to ask directions to the nearest auto wrecker, or to borrow a respectable wardrobe.

There was another bang at the door, followed by a man's impatient voice. "Come on, Miss McKinley. I know you're here."

Christine's stomach fluttered with alarm, and she spread her hand over it. So much for the asking-for-directions theory.

Suddenly, coming out here didn't seem as brilliant an idea as it had two days ago. Then, she'd just wanted to go someplace quiet and safe, where she could relax and figure out what was going on. Her condo in Florida didn't meet those requirements. The family home in Calgary had been sold after Christine's father passed away. Her mother had moved into an apartment, but she wasn't there right now; she was spending the summer in France with Keith. Christine had briefly considered joining them, then decided that traipsing around a foreign country, studying medieval architecture, was no way to deal with her problem. The family ski chalet, currently owned by Keith, had seemed like a better solution.

Now it seemed less like a solution and more like a really bad idea. There was no phone here. The nearest police station was miles away. There were hardly any neighbors, and the ones there probably knew more about ski wax and Lycra than they did about self-defense.

The man knocked again. There was silence, accompanied by Christine's almost audible heartbeats. He might not be dangerous, but Christine couldn't think of a safe way to find out. She wasn't about to open the door and politely ask if he was here to do her in.

He banged once more. Then the doorknob began to turn.

Christine watched it in mesmerized horror. How strong was that lock? Could he...?

He couldn't. The doorknob rattled again. Then there was the creak of wooden stairs, followed by unmistakable sounds of footsteps heading not toward the car, but toward the back of the cottage.

Christine frantically ran through her options. Her rental car was parked back there. It couldn't be seen from the road, but that man would see it as soon as he rounded the corner. Then he'd know for certain she was here. She could just stay inside and...

And what? Hope he'd go away. What if he didn't?

Christine took a deep breath and raised her chin.

She wasn't going to just cower in here. She was going to find out what was going on, and she was not, repeat not, going to get killed in the process.

She tiptoed toward the back door, where she'd placed her green-and-gray golf bag.

Which club would be best for a hit man? A nine iron?

Or the graphite-shaft, metal three wood?

WAS THIS WHERE Chrissy McKinley was hiding out?

Alec O'Brian strolled around the side of the deserted-looking cottage, checking for some sign of life. He wouldn't be surprised if Chrissy wasn't here. After all, there wasn't a bean sprout in sight—or a golf course, either. However, when Chrissy had abruptly canceled all her scheduled public appearances and dropped out of sight, he'd suspected she might be headed for home. There was no one at either her mother's or her brother's place, but when he'd ferreted out the information that her brother owned a ski chalet, he'd decided to check it out.

Normally Alec didn't go to this much trouble to get material for his sports column. He didn't usually bother with retired professional athletes, either, especially when the career they'd retired from was golf! However, Chrissy McKinley's recent peculiar behavior had him curious.

Christine McKinley had been a minor sensation a few years ago, when she'd been playing professional golf. She'd won a fair number of tournaments, although the last two years she'd played she'd been less than spectacular. She'd finally left the sport a couple of years ago, to take a marketing position with HoleSum Foods, a U.S.-based health-food company.

Alec had always suspected Chrissy's retirement had more to do with her nerves than with a deep desire to sell health food. She'd been one of those athletes who took her sport far too seriously. As a matter of fact, she was one of the most driven players he'd ever seen.

And, actually, he'd seen her play quite often. That wasn't because he was fascinated by professional female golfers. He wasn't. They were a well-mannered, well-dressed bunch—not bad qualities, perhaps, but not something that made for good copy. However, Chrissy had been born and raised in Calgary, so there was a great deal of local interest in her. Because of this, Alec had made a small effort to follow her career. He'd even interviewed her a few times, and saw her every so often at local charity events. She was a slender redhead, with a figure as uninspired as her game and a manner that was as controlled and introverted in person as it had been on the golf course.

Recently Chrissy had started acting peculiar. First she'd claimed a car had tried to run her down in a hotel parking lot. Then she'd insisted she'd found a man in her condo, although there was no evidence to substantiate that. Finally, last week, during a charity golf tournament in Colorado, some no-brained yahoo had fired a gun, and Christine had gone ballistic.

No one had suggested that that gun had been aimed at Christine—or anyone else in particular. The gunman had evaded capture, but the general consensus was that he was simply an idiot trying to stir up trouble.

That wasn't Miss McKinley's theory, though. She'd suggested to the police that she was the intended victim. Then she'd canceled her scheduled public appearances and had dropped out of sight.

Her actions had taken everyone by surprise, including Alec. The most emotion he'd seen Chrissy exhibit was a tight-lipped frown when things weren't going her way. Were those nerves of hers giving her problems again? Or was this whole thing a new marketing strategy of HoleSum Foods?

Alec was unusually curious about it. He rounded the back corner of the cottage, experiencing a small surge of satisfaction as he caught sight of the pale green sedan parked behind it. Someone was definitely here.

He took a step toward it. As he did, something hard tangled with his ankles. Alec struggled to maintain his balance, failed and fell headlong into the mud. His sunglasses bounced off his nose, and when he tried to grab them, both they and his hand landed in the mud as well. "Damn!"

"Don't move," warned a female voice.

Alec glanced to his right and found himself staring at a pair of white knees. His gaze traveled up the legs to the brown shorts, then to a beige sweatshirt, and finally to the face of the gray-eyed woman standing beside him. She had shoulder-length red hair that was falling out of a loosely pinned barrette at the side of her head. Her hands were clutched around a golf club that was aimed directly at his head. "Don't move," she warned again. "I've got a three wood and I know how to..."

Her voice trailed off as their gazes met. Her eyes widened with recognition.

Alec suddenly remembered every word he'd written about this woman.

Our own Chrissy McKinley relived her tendency to choke under pressure, blowing an easy two-foot putt to place seventh. You're still in the money, Chrissy, babe. Couldn't you muster up one tiny smile?

Perhaps Chrissy McKinley should try wearing short shorts. It might not improve her game, but it could make it more fun to watch.

You can either watch Chrissy McKinley meander down the green or catch celebrity trout fishing on cable. The celebes will be more interesting, folks.

He ducked.

"IT'S NOT ENTIRELY my fault," Christine said defensively.

She studied the man now attempting to wipe the

mud off his jacket, unsure whether she felt relieved or dismayed by his identity. At least he wasn't a crazed killer here to do her in. On the other hand, he wasn't exactly one of the good guys, either. "You were sneaking around," she continued. "And—"

"I was sneaking around?" Alec O'Brian's eyes were a lively combination of brilliant blue and sparkling green. Right now, the blue part showed avid curiosity, while the green portion hinted strongly at amusement. "What do you call what you were doing?" He gave his jacket a final swipe and straightened. "Is that the way you usually greet visitors? Or is it something you do just for me?"

Christine's spine stiffened indignantly. "No, of course not. I had no idea who you were. I—"

"There are other ways of discerning a person's identity." One side of his mouth rose in a wicked half smirk. "You could, for example, have opened the door and asked."

Christine shifted uncomfortably and tried not to stare at his face. There were several things wrong with Alec O'Brian, but his looks weren't one of them. Even now, with mud streaked down his cheek and a chin that hadn't fraternized with a razor for a good two days, he was immensely good-looking. "There's no need to be sarcastic," she admonished. "I've already apologized."

"I don't call 'oh, sorry' an adequate apology for a brutal attack on my bod." He leered suggestively.

"However, I can think of a few ways you can make it up to me."

Christine tightened her grip on the three wood, along with her lips. He was getting a real kick out of this, wasn't he? "What are you doing here, Mr. O'Brian?"

Alec rolled his eyes toward the heavens. "I'm a reporter, Chrissy. What do you think I'm doing here?"

Christine sighed heavily and glanced around for inspiration on how to handle this. She'd never suspected her mysterious visitor might be from the press. Even during her more famous years reporters hadn't paid that much attention to her—and they'd never made any attempt to track her down. She really wished this one hadn't bothered.

She refocused on his face. "How did you find me?"

"Incredible intelligence, outstanding charm and fifty bucks." His teeth flashed white against his tanned face as he grinned. "How about if we finish this conversation inside? It must be drier, it has to be warmer and I'd like to clean up a little."

Christine hesitated, then reluctantly nodded. She didn't want him inside, but the mud on him was her fault. She could scarcely deny him the opportunity to wash up. "Of course. Come in."

"Thanks." He shoved his hands into his jacket pockets and wandered toward the cottage, with Christine trailing after him.

She made a face at his back. If she had to pick someone to demonstrate her paranoia to, she really wished she'd picked someone else. It wasn't that she had anything against reporters. Some of them were actually quite nice people. Alec O'Brian just didn't fall into that category. His column was gossipy, rude, chauvinistic and, unfortunately, extremely readable. Any comment he'd made about her had been less than complimentary—and that was before she'd aimed a golf club at his head.

Normally Christine wouldn't have bothered reading what he wrote. However, her own mother was an Alec O'Brian fan. She also thought any mention of Christine had to be saved for posterity. She had carefully clipped out every one of his comments, highlighted it in fluorescent pink marker and placed it in a scrapbook. Her doing so was very sweet, but every time Christine opened the book, she would read that condescending "Chrissy" and her jaw would start aching.

Alec removed his shoes at the door and strolled down the hall to the bathroom. Christine rested her back against the kitchen counter, feeling a little light-headed from all the excitement. It was too bad she didn't have a photograph of Alec cowering in the mud at her feet. It would definitely improve her scrapbook.

She giggled at the thought, then almost immediately sobered. She might have derived a small amount of satisfaction from seeing Alec down in the mud, but he could very well even the score—and then some—in his column. There wasn't much she could say in her own defense, either. She could scarcely tell Alec O'Brian that she'd attacked him because her left thumb had twitched.

"I don't suppose you've got a beer in that fridge?" Alec asked.

Christine glanced across the room. He was lounging in the kitchen doorway, one wide shoulder braced against the doorjamb. He'd removed his blazer, along with the grime on his face, but he still looked something like a well-built, slightly amused pirate. The clothes that had appeared shabby earlier made him look carelessly masculine.

Her gaze traveled down his body. According to the rumors she'd heard, Alec spent more time carousing than he did reporting. If that were true, the effects of the carousing didn't show on him. His stomach was flat, his tanned arms firm and muscled, and the pant-leg stretched over one thigh indicated that it wasn't flabby, either.

Christine followed the line of his thigh a little higher, realized what portion of his anatomy she was staring at and jerked her gaze back to his face. "I'm afraid not. I don't drink. Listen, I—"

"You're more the tofu-and-goat's-milk type, I suppose." He straightened, muscle by muscle, in a movement that was just as distracting as the rest of his appearance. "What about your roommate? Is he into goat's milk as well?"

"Roommate?" Christine echoed. "I don't—"

"Surely you're not here all alone?" Alec took a look down the hall, as if expecting to see another person materialize. "Isn't there some guy hot for your bod hanging around?"

Christine shook her head. There hadn't been a man in her life for some time. Normally that didn't bother her, but now that he mentioned it, she wouldn't mind having some strong, macho guy materialize in the hall.

"Why not?" Alec put his head to one side and examined her up and down. "You're attractive enough—in a respectable way, of course. You even look good in those shorts you've got on. They're too long and too loose, but they do sort of suit you."

Christine wasn't sure if that was a compliment or not. "Oh," she said. "Well, uh…"

"They don't suit most people," Alec reflected. "I think it's because of the knees. Most people don't have great knees." He ambled across the kitchen to sprawl in a white wooden chair beside the table. "That's why women should wear short, tight shorts. It gives you something to look at other than their knees." His gaze honed in on her legs. "Not that there's anything wrong with yours."

Christine suddenly felt underdressed and a bit too warm. She drew in a breath, which failed to cool her down. His movements had caused his scent to swirl around the room—a musky mixture of whiskey, smoke, sweat and maleness that evoked images of hot nights and wrinkled sheets.

She impatiently shoved those thoughts away and watched him stretch his legs out in front of him. Obviously, letting him in had been very poor strategy. Now that he was here, it wasn't going to be easy to get him out.

Christine tried anyway. "Listen, I really don't want—"

"To be interviewed?" Alec chose an apple from the bowl on the table. "I figured as much, since it was so hard to find you." He sank his teeth into the apple. "Why is that, by the way? How come you're hiding out here all by yourself?"

Christine watched the juice spurt out of the apple and her own mouth watered. "I'm not exactly hiding," she lied. "I'm just, uh, taking a vacation."

"At a ski resort?" Alec crunched the apple between his teeth. "Isn't August a bad time to take up skiing?"

"I don't ski," Christine murmured, mesmerized by the way his tanned fingers curled around the fruit. "I did when I was younger, but..." She realized what she was saying and gave her head an impatient shake. "I'm not here to ski. I'm just, um, taking a few days off."

Alec studied her face. "You do look as if you could use a vacation," he agreed. "What's the problem,

Chrissy? The strain of hocking bean sprouts getting on your nerves?''

Christine's spine stiffened. "I do *not* hock bean sprouts. And there is nothing wrong with my nerves!''

"There isn't?'' He opened his eyes very wide. "I thought that was the reason you've been acting so bizarre lately.''

"I haven't been acting bizarre,'' Christine insisted. "I—''

"Yeah, you have. A couple of weeks ago you were telling the world that someone tried to turn you into roadkill in a parking lot.''

"They did. I—''

"You're sure about that?'' He grinned, and the dimple in his left cheek flashed. "According to witnesses, the car was just swerving through the parking lot. Yet you claimed it was aiming at you.''

Christine squirmed. At the time, she had thought the dark sedan *was* aiming for her. "I, uh...''

"Then there was the 'man in my condo' thing. You ran into the street, screaming at the top of your lungs that a man was in your place. But when they checked, no one was there, and there was no sign of a forced entry.''

"I saw someone there.'' She had seen someone—at least, she thought she had.

"And finally we've got that charity thing the other day.'' He aimed the half-eaten apple at her in accusatory fashion. "Some no-brain fired a gun and you went ballistic."

Christine flicked back her hair. "I did *not* go ballistic. I simply got out of the way."

His eyes brimmed with amusement. "You did more than get out of the way. You screamed and dropped to the ground like a stone."

Christine was positive her face was bright red. "It was a normal reaction!" she retorted. "What would you do if someone fired a gun in your presence? Stand very still to make sure he didn't miss?"

"I don't know, since it's never happened." Alec folded his hand into a fist and scrubbed it down the side of his face while he thought about it. "I imagine I'd react in such a brave, macho fashion that I'd completely ignore the risk to myself, easily disarm the man and overpower him with a strong uppercut." He grinned. "Of course, I'd have to be really drunk to even consider trying it."

"I'm sure that's not a problem for you," Christine muttered.

He chuckled. "I admit I've had a little practice. However, I'm willing to bet you haven't. Maybe it's something you should try. It might help you relax. Get you over this paranoia thing."

Christine narrowed her eyes until he was no more than a blurry figure. "I do not have any sort of a thing!"

"That's how it looks." He finished the apple, seeds

and all, then wiped his hands on his thighs. "Didn't you tell the police that bullet was meant for you?"

"No! I *asked* the police if there was any chance that maniac was aiming at me." She shuddered slightly as she recalled the scene. The police had been about as understanding as Alec. "It's a perfectly logical question. When someone shoots a gun in your presence, you want to know if he was shooting at you."

"No one else asked that. Besides, you weren't the only VIP in the vicinity. There were a ton of celebrities around."

The police had mentioned that as well. Apparently, they considered the mayor and a senator better candidates for assassination than the spokesperson of a health-food company. Normally Christine would have agreed with them, but in this case…

Alec folded his arms on the table. "Why would you even suggest that the bullet had your name on it?"

Because my left thumb twitched! Christine pressed her lips together to keep from shouting that out. Alec looked amused enough as it was. If she told him that, he'd probably burst into gales of laughter. Then he'd inform the entire world that she was a lunatic. That would do nothing for either her career or her reputation.

"Well?" he urged. "Is there someone out there with a deep, dark motive for getting rid of you?"

Christine had spent a lot of time wondering about that herself. "I don't think…"

"Neither do I," Alec agreed. "Unless a group of dedicated chocoholics decided they'd had enough of those health-food commercials."

Christine didn't say anything. He was right. No one would hurt her because of her work with HoleSum Foods.

"And I doubt there's a dastardly villain in your past," Alec continued. "You were hardly worth taking out when you were playing professionally."

Christine bristled at that. "I won—"

"You didn't win anything the last couple of years you played. It seems to me you had a hard enough time just making the cut."

Oh, shut up, Christine thought resentfully. She folded her hands in front of her and studied them. She was not going to throw the entire contents of the fruit bowl in his face. She was not.

She gritted her teeth, ignored the ache in her jaw and produced a cool smile. "Isn't there some celebrity trout fishing you should be observing right now? I'm sure it would be more interesting—"

"I find paranoia very interesting."

"I am *not* paranoid!"

"What are you then?" Alec prodded. "Three times you've claimed someone was trying to get you. You can't think of a reason why someone would want you to leave the planet. But you're still hiding out up here, attacking whoever shows up. Sounds like someone with unreasonable fears to me." He paused. "Or is this just an attempt to get your name in the paper again—along with a little publicity for that nutritionally correct company you work for?"

Did he really thing HoleSum Foods would benefit from having its spokesperson acting like a nervous wreck? "Don't be ridiculous!"

"Or maybe it's an excuse for that horrible game you played the other day?" Alec offered. "It's a good thing it was just for charity. If that's how you'd played on the tour, you would have starved to death."

My thumb didn't twitch when I was on the tour! Christine mentally shouted. She bit on her lip and swallowed. "I was a little unnerved by that shooting, I suppose, and—"

"A little unnerved?" Alec echoed incredulously. "Now there's an original statement." His lips curled upward, his eyes sparkled merrily and everything about him suggested laughter. "Can I quote you on that?"

Someday Christine would probably look back on this and laugh, as well. However, today wasn't the day. "You can't quote me on anything!" She bounced to her feet, anxious to get him out of the house before she really did start throwing things. "It's time for you to leave, Mr. O'Brian."

Alec's smile widened. "Don't get mad now, Chrissy. I—"

"I am *not* mad!" Christine clenched her teeth. "I am simply asking you to leave."

His smile remained, his good humor apparently undaunted by her anger. "I don't have much of a story. What do you want me to say? That you're paranoid? Or that you're up here trying to get over being paranoid?"

"I don't want you to say anything except good-bye!"

"I can't promise that." He rose to his feet and picked up his jacket. "You've still got a few fans out there, Chrissy. They want to know what's going on with you."

"I am taking a vacation! That's all that is going on with me."

"You can't enjoy a vacation all by yourself." He shoved his feet into his shoes. "Maybe you should have a little company—to take your mind off your problems."

Christine opened and closed her mouth, but no sound came out.

"I'd be willing to volunteer my services," Alec offered. He rested his back against the wall and gave her a head-to-toe assessment that left no doubt about what he was suggesting. "I can guarantee you won't have opportunity to be paranoid with me around."

That was probably true, Christine decided. She'd probably murder him long before paranoia set in. "I don't need any company, Mr. O'Brian—certainly not yours!" She marched to the front door and yanked it open. "Goodbye!"

Alec chuckled and followed. He stopped right in front of her, standing so close they were almost touching. "Bye, Chrissy. Take care of yourself." He patted her cheek. "Oh...one more thing."

She slapped his hand away. "What?"

"You do have great knees." He grinned cheerfully and wandered out, leaving Christine glaring furiously at his back.

2

"A MORE SERIOUS APPROACH?" Alec echoed.

He took a long sip of coffee from the mug in his hand and eyed his boss over the rim. Harper Brandt looked more like a Mafia godfather than the managing editor of a daily newspaper. He had the bulky build, the blue pin-striped suits and the pearl gray eyes.

He was also highly dedicated to his job. Alec didn't mind that. He just wished Harper would save his "serious journalism" lectures for the hard-news boys and leave the sports department alone. "We have this conversation every two weeks, Harp, and I still don't know what it's about. I write a sports column. Sports are games, and games are supposed to be fun. They are not supposed to be reported with a 'serious approach.'"

Harper settled his bulk more comfortably into his chair and spoke in a gravelly half whisper that was somehow audible in spite of the clatter and commotion of the city newsroom on the other side of the closed door. "They're also not supposed to be treated like idle gossip."

"Gossip?"

"That's what you're writing now!" Harper accused. "Even you have to admit you don't put a lot of effort into producing that column. You attend some sporting event, have a few drinks with the players and fans afterward, then dump whatever comes into your brain into your word processor. You expend more effort having a good time than you do working for me."

Alec shrugged. That was a fairly accurate description of how he produced his column. Still, he didn't see what that had to do with anything. "The reading public doesn't seem to be objecting."

"I'm objecting. It's not good journalism. I'd like to see something with a little more depth than locker-room gossip, your opinion of the quarterback's performance and a critique of the cheerleaders' outfits!"

"I didn't critique them! I merely suggested they should show a little more leg." Harper's expression darkened further, and Alec sighed. "Come on, Harp, I write about other things. Just yesterday I did that piece on Chrissy McKinley."

"That McKinley piece is a good example of what I'm talking about. You went to all the trouble of tracking her down." He eyed Alec suspiciously. "You did track her down, didn't you? Or did you merely stumble across her in a bar?"

"Not quite. I had to do a little digging."

"Probably very little," Harper guessed accurately.

"However, even a little effort from you is something of an accomplishment, I suppose." His gaze sharpened. "But you didn't dig deep enough. You could have done something with a little more depth."

"Depth?" Alec gave his head a slight shake in a vain attempt to make sense out of Harper's words. "You want me to write something deep about health food?"

Harper's face reddened. "I wasn't referring to health food. I was speaking of the McKinley woman. She is a public figure. There could be something to these things she claimed happened to her."

Alec rolled his eyes. "You don't believe that any more than I do! Chrissy is a little stressed out, that's all. And you know why she's like that? It's because she takes a 'serious approach.' Next thing you know, she'll be wearing a pin-striped suit and telling other people to sober up, too."

Harper's lips tightened. "Let's terminate this discussion before my stress level gives me a heart attack." He gestured toward the door. "And I want to see some serious material in your column in the near future."

"I'll give it serious consideration," Alec advised. He grinned at the string of foul language that followed this announcement and ambled out the door.

His smile faded as he settled into his own cubicle. He might not agree with Harper's "serious approach" stuff, but the man was right in one respect.

Alec didn't put a lot of effort into producing his column.

He picked up a pencil and absently twirled it between his fingers. It hadn't always been this easy. When he'd first started his journalism career, he had given it all he had. Over the years, he'd drifted into his current mode of operation.

Harper had no reason to complain, though. Alec's column was a popular feature of the sports section. And although Alec felt guilty every so often about his lack of dedication, he knew there was no reason to feel that way. The reading public liked his work just as much as they had when he had toiled at it. There was no point in going to a lot of trouble to produce pretty much the same reaction.

As for this Chrissy McKinley stuff, Harper was really out to lunch about that. Alec had always suspected Chrissy had a problem with nerves, and this just proved him right. She was like a lot of other professional athletes. They threw themselves into what they did so completely that they forgot to enjoy themselves. They were playing a game that was supposed to be fun! If they'd lighten up, they'd probably play a lot better.

That was Chrissy's problem. She was obviously on edge, which came from taking things so seriously. It was too bad she was like that. A woman with knees like hers—

Alec tossed the pencil onto his desk, exasperated

with himself for the thought. Chrissy was a pleasant-looking woman, but there wasn't anything outstanding about her. She had ordinary features, gray eyes and a clear, clean complexion. Her figure was nothing to write home about, either. However, those knees of hers had crossed his mind more than once since he'd left her place yesterday afternoon. Along with the knees came a mental image of how she might look when she was as bare as they'd been.

Alec impatiently shoved the picture out of his mind. He wasn't interested in Chrissy McKinley! He preferred agreeable, aggressive women, who pretty much invited themselves into his bed without him having to do much about getting them there. There were plenty of those around. He didn't have to bother with a serious, stressed-out health-food addict, no matter how attractive her knees were.

"I'M FINE," Christine insisted.

She held the pay phone close to one ear, while pressing a palm to the other in order to block out the noise from the busy Banff street. "I'm furious, but I'm fine."

"Oh?" Estelle's raspy voice was so clear that she could easily be in the next phone booth, instead of in Florida. "Who are you…?"

"Alec O'Brian!" Christine practically spat his name. "He's a sportswriter for the *Calgary Daily Centennial*. I think I've mentioned him a couple of times.

He tracked me down, and you should hear what he said about me!" She pulled the folded newspaper out of her purse and gave it an angry shake. "'All of you Chrissy McKinley fans will be pleased to know that Miss McKinley is alive and well, and showing off those wicked knees—'"

"Knees?" Estelle interrupted. "What...?"

Christine flushed as she thought about Alec's gaze resting on her knees. "He's got some weird thing about knees. Where was I?" She continued reading. "'...wicked knees close to her hometown of Calgary.

"'For those of you who blinked and missed it, Chrissy McKinley spent a few unexciting years on the professional golfing circuit, highlighted by a win in the U.S. Open. These days she's better known as the earnest face on those HoleSum Foods labels.

"'Apparently hocking bean sprouts isn't any easier on Chrissy's nerves than professional golf. Over the last couple of months, she has claimed that someone tried to run her over, that a stranger was in her apartment and that she was shot at. None of these incidents could be verified.

"'Presently, Chrissy is taking a few days off. But a ski resort in August strikes this reporter as an odd place to spend a vacation. However, peace and quiet and fresh air might be just what Chrissy needs to recover. Hopefully, it will also improve her disposition, which seems to be as temperamental as her two-foot putts used to be.'"

"Well!" Estelle exclaimed.

"Well, indeed." Christine shoved the paper back into the side pocket of her purse. "I don't hock bean sprouts, there isn't anything wrong with my nerves, I have a lovely disposition and I really wish he'd stop referring to me as 'Chrissy'!"

"I wouldn't take any notice of it," Estelle advised. "All sports reporters are textbook underachievers. They are unable to do anything themselves, so they try to boost their egos by putting down those who have succeeded. It's classic."

"It is?" Alec hadn't seemed like someone in dire need of an ego boost. As a matter of fact, his ego had appeared to be in as good a shape as the rest of him.

"So?" Estelle prompted. "What are your plans now?"

Christine deliberately misunderstood. "I'm going shopping. I'm already in Banff. I drove here to get a newspaper and see what Mr. O'Brian had to say. Now that I'm in town, I might as well enjoy myself."

"That's not what I meant. I was wondering where you're going to go now. You can't stay there. Mr. O'Brian didn't specifically mention Calypso Canyon, but it wouldn't be difficult for someone else to figure it out."

A cold shiver wended its way up Christine's spine. "It doesn't matter who figures it out," she said stoutly. "I'm sure there aren't that many reporters interested in me." She drew in a breath. "And I'm sure no one else is, either."

Estelle sounded startled by that. "You are?"

Actually, Christine wasn't one hundred percent convinced, but she didn't want to tell Estelle that. "Yes, I am. Those things that happened to me must have just been accidents. After all, there's no reason for anyone to want to hurt me." Alec was right about that. She wasn't important enough to bump off.

Estelle was silent. Christine waited for a moment, then went on talking. "As for this thing with my thumb, well, it's probably nothing. After all, it twitched when Alec showed up, and all he wanted to do was talk to me." *And write an article about her that told the immediate world where to find her.* Christine shoved that thought away. It didn't matter who knew where she was. No one was after her. "I have been busy lately," she added. "Maybe I do need a few days off."

"You need more than a few days off!" Estelle exclaimed. "Your symptoms suggest you may be suffering from compulsive chronic memory syndrome. I've done extensive research on the subject and I believe..."

Christine rested a shoulder against the Plexiglas and sighed as Estelle rambled on. They had been friends for years, and Christine was very fond of her. However, she did have a few theories Christine didn't agree with. This compulsive-syndrome thing was one of them. "I don't think that's my problem."

"You can't rule it out. Compulsive chronic memory syndrome is similar to suppressed memory syndrome. However, in those cases the trauma is caused by a particular event. A child who was attacked by a dog could, as an adult, feel fearful and threatened by something as simple as seeing an animal, even though he or she couldn't recall the attack."

Christine knew very little about the inner workings of the human brain. "I don't see…"

Estelle warmed to her topic. "My research suggests that stressful events may have the same effect. The stress itself becomes a suppressed memory. That's compulsive chronic memory syndrome."

"That's, uh, fascinating, but—"

"A good percentage of professional athletes probably suffer from this. The stress of competition becomes a suppressed memory. Exposure to the same conditions triggers a feeling of being in danger."

"But I'm not exposed to the same conditions," Christine objected. "I haven't played professionally for years. Besides, I wasn't that stressed out about it when I was doing it. Why would I get stressed out about it now?"

"It's in your subconscious! If you'd just come here, we could do a proper diagnosis. A little biofeedback analysis, hypnosis, relaxation therapy… In a few months, you'd—"

"I'm not coming there!" Christine realized she'd practically shouted and bit her lip. Estelle was just trying to help, but the last thing Christine wanted to do was spend weeks sequestered in the Lamont Sports Psychology Clinic while a dozen psychiatrists plumbed her psyche. She didn't have anything against therapy, but she didn't believe it was necessary for her. "I can't come there now. We've got a store opening in Chicago in a couple of weeks. I have to be there. Then there's the charity tournament in Vermont, the workshop I'm giving in Seattle next month and—"

"Your health is more important—"

"My health is fine!" Christine recalled her attack on Alec and winced. "At least it had better be. My contract with HoleSum is up the end of September. They won't renew if I don't properly represent their product."

"I'm sure they'll understand. And—"

"No, they won't. And what about the sports program for inner-city children I've been trying to arrange? I've got some interested sponsors. I don't want them to back out at the last minute because I'm acting like a nervous wreck!"

"That's not—"

"Besides, Estelle, I just can't have people saying this about me! I didn't stop golfing because of nerves and I'm not going to stop doing this because of them, either. There is nothing wrong with me! I need a few days off, that's all. I'm going to spend a couple of days at Keith's cottage, just like I planned. Then I'm going back to work. And if this thing with my thumb happens again, I'm just going to ignore it."

"You can't ignore it!" Estelle exclaimed. "Your body is trying to tell you something. Ignoring it could be dangerous to your mental well-being." She softened her tone. "I'm your friend, Christine. I also happen to be a psychiatrist. And I think you need professional help. I'm sorry, but I do."

"I don't." Christine didn't want to argue about this anymore. "I appreciate your concern and support, but I think this is something I have to do alone."

ALEC THOUGHT she needed company. Estelle thought she need a psychologist. Christine didn't think she needed either. However, when she pulled the car into the lane behind the cottage a few hours later, she found herself wishing she had the companionship.

She switched off the car engine and sat for a moment looking at the dark cottage. She didn't often feel lonely, but during her day of shopping—despite how enjoyable it had been—she had found herself envying the couples and groups she'd seen.

She sighed and gathered up her parcels. The eight years she'd spent golfing professionally hadn't left much time to establish relationships. The past two hadn't been much better. She'd accepted the job with HoleSum not only because she firmly believed in the benefits of good nutrition, but also because she believed in the charities they supported. She attended charity tournaments across the country, gave clinics sponsored by HoleSum, made public appearances at stores carrying HoleSum products. She might meet a lot of people, but she didn't have that many close friends.

As for men, well, that was practically impossible. Her last romantic relationship had ended a year ago, mainly because of her schedule.

Christine resolutely climbed out of the car. She didn't need anyone else to help her get over this crisis. She was quite capable of doing it by herself. And if a few more nosy reporters did show up, she'd handle them in a cool, civilized manner. As for a potential killer, well, she was positive one didn't exist.

Well, almost positive.

Christine shuddered involuntarily. Estelle was right. It wouldn't take reporters long to find this place, and it wouldn't take anyone else long, either.

It didn't matter who found her, she assured herself. There was no potential killer. Still, she felt uneasy as she walked to the back door. The dark cottage and the sound of the wind in the trees increased her discomfort. To make matters worse, as soon as she placed the key into the lock, her left thumb gave a slight, involuntary twitch.

Christine stared at it for a moment while her heart

rate increased. "A twitching thumb means nothing," she announced out loud. "It's just stress."

She took a deep breath, opened the door and stepped inside.

Her thumb twitched again.

Christine curled her hand into a fist and switched on a light. The place looked exactly the way she'd left it. She took a few more steps, turned on the kitchen light and set her bags on the table. "See?" she said cheerfully. "Nothing is wrong." She slowly uncurled her fist and looked down at her thumb.

It twitched again.

"Oh, for heaven sakes!" She marched determinedly through the cottage, switching on lights as she went. There wasn't one single thing out of place, the front door was still locked and there was no sign that anyone had been here since she'd left. Still, her heart was pounding and she felt as terrified as she'd felt at that charity tournament. Every single nerve in her body was shouting at her to get out of that cottage as soon as possible.

Christine stood in the living room and tried to talk herself out of it. She was being silly. She was imagining things. She...

Her thumb twitched again.

She was going to get out of there, right now! Christine snatched up her purse and dashed toward the back door. No matter how ridiculous it was, no matter how paranoid she was acting, she could not stay

in this place one more second without either screaming or throwing up!

She ran outside, stumbling through the darkening
night, tripping over stumps and roots in her haste.

When she was a hundred yards from the cottage,
she stopped and turned around. There was no sound.
The cottage looked very innocent and very safe.

"Maybe I had better see Estelle," Christine muttered. "I am acting crazy."

She took a couple of deep breaths, then sheepishly
began to walk back toward the cottage.

There was an enormous bang. Christine stopped
dead and watched in horrified disbelief as the cottage
went up in a tremendous burst of flame.

"Oh my," she murmured. She held her left hand
up to her face and slowly flexed her thumb. Her
twitching thumb *wasn't* a sign of stress! It was a warning. It meant she was in danger.

Which meant she'd been in danger all those other
times, as well. "Congratulations, Chrissy," she whispered to herself. "You aren't crazy. Someone really is
trying to kill you."

3

"DAMN," Alec muttered.

He frowned down at his jacket pocket, which was making a loud buzzing noise, then turned his attention back to the screen on the other side of the sports bar. It was the second overtime inning, score tied, bases loaded, two men out...and the agreeably aggressive blonde beside him had her hand on his thigh.

It was no time to take a phone call.

His jacket pocket buzzed again. His cellular phone. He must have forgotten to turn that darn thing off.

He tried to ignore it, failed and finally pulled it out of his pocket. "O'Brian," he grunted into it.

"Sparks," growled the voice of the night editor, identifying himself. "And before you start whining, this isn't my idea. Harper told me to call you."

The blonde inched her chair closer. The Mets pulled their pitcher. "What?" Alec asked.

"There's a fire...."

"A fire?" Alec frowned at the phone. "This is Alec O'Brian, Mike. I write a sports column."

"I know who you are. I—"

"Fire isn't a sport." Alec took a look at the almost

unbelievable bustline of the blonde. She smiled invitingly and her fingers inched higher. "Fire is a chemical reaction...."

"Will you shut up and listen? This involves the McKinley dame—the one you interviewed the other day."

Great. Now he was compelled to check out the blonde's knees. They didn't look soft and smooth and sexy. As a matter of fact, they looked distinctly fleshy. "What about her?"

"That place she's staying at in Calypso Canyon blew up."

Alec forgot all about the Mets game and the blonde. "Blew up?" he repeated hoarsely.

"Blew up...burned up. Something."

A jumble of horrible images flashed across Alec's brain. "And Chrissy...uh, Miss McKinley?"

"Apparently no one was injured." Mike paused. "I know this isn't your usual thing, but Harper suggested you might want to cover—since you talked to her the other day. I've sent the photographer out, and if you're not going, I can..."

Alec squinted at the television, where the Mets' recently acquired rookie pitcher was walking out to the mound. Alec eyed the blonde, almost groaning out loud as her fingers tightened. He didn't need to make the hour-and-a-half drive to Calypso Canyon. It was more of a news story than a sports story. No one was injured.

Still, he found himself mentally saying goodbye to both the blonde and the Mets. "No," he told Mike. "I'd better handle it."

He reset the phone, astonishing himself by his actions, and regretfully removed the blonde's hand. He was giving up all this to check on a skinny redhead with a touchy disposition and sexy knees? What next? Was he going to start wearing pin-striped suits and telling other guys to get serious?

He mumbled an excuse to the blonde and wandered out to his car. Maybe Chrissy wasn't the only one who needed a vacation.

THERE WERE A FEW good things about being a local celebrity, Christine decided.

One was that some people were very, very nice to you.

She sat on the bed in one of the examining rooms of the small Banff hospital. It was extremely white and extremely quiet—a welcome change from the dark, the smoke and all the commotion her fire had created.

It certainly had caused a commotion. Another resident of Calypso Canyon had materialized soon after the explosion. He'd contacted the authorities, while Christine remained outside the cottage, having some vague notion of directing the firefighters to the blaze.

Then an avalanche of people and equipment had descended. There had been firefighters, police officers, helicopters, reporters, TV cameras.... Christine had assured the firefighters that there were no people trapped inside. Then she'd stood, shivering and watching, until someone had draped a blanket over her shoulders and led her into an ambulance.

She looked around the room, wishing she'd had the presence of mind to rescue some of Keith's belongings when she'd raced out of the cottage. Now all his stuff was burned to smithereens, along with her golf clubs. Fortunately, he'd been more concerned about her than the loss of his possessions.

So had her mother. They'd both immediately offered to return home—an offer Christine had rejected. She hadn't mentioned to them that she suspected her life was in danger. There was no point. She doubted either her sixty-year-old mother or her scholarly brother would know any more about how to deal with this situation than she did. Besides, she didn't want them to get caught up in whatever was going on.

She'd also spoken with Estelle. Christine grimaced as she recalled that conversation. In spite of everything that had happened, her friend insisted that Christine's life was not in danger. Estelle had tried once again to convince her to come to her clinic and had even been prepared to fly up and make all the arrangements. Christine had left the conversation with a vague "I'll think about it." She didn't know what she was going to do, but she was positive the Lamont Clinic didn't figure into her plans.

The door swung open. Christine looked up, antici-
pating a medical figure of some sort to take her to her
room. She'd already been examined by a doctor, who
had pronounced her healthy, but suffering from
shock. He'd sympathetically suggested that she
spend the night in the hospital, so they could keep an
eye on her. Christine suspected he was simply being
kind, but she wasn't going to argue. She didn't have
any place to go. She didn't have any way to get there,
either, since her rental car had been totaled in the fire.

The sandy-haired man now closing the door behind him wasn't dressed like a health professional.
He had on blue jeans with holes in the knees, a gray
T-shirt and a black blazer. Christine's gaze traveled
from his attire up to his stubbled chin and large
green-and-blue eyes. "So this is where you're hiding
this time," he said.

For a moment she was actually glad to see him,
simply because he had a familiar face. Then she realized who he was, and the probable reason for his
presence, and her pleasure evaporated. "How did
you get in here?" she demanded. "They're not letting
reporters—"

"I know." Alec rested his back against the door.
"They're being incredibly difficult about it. They
wouldn't let me see you until I told them I was a
friend of yours."

Christine was outraged. "A friend?"

"That's right. They were pathetically glad to hear

that. I think they were relieved to know you had friends." He eyed her up and down and his expression darkened to concern. "What are you doing in a hospital, Chrissy? You didn't get singed in that fire, did you?"

Christine wasn't sure which was harder to take—the concern on his face, which she knew was assumed, or the fact that there was no one around whose concern would be genuine. "No," she said crisply. "They're just keeping me here for observation."

Alec nodded wisely. "That's probably a good idea. You don't look too good."

Christine hadn't imagined she looked her best. However, she couldn't look any more scruffy than he did. Unfortunately, scruffy suited him, and she knew it didn't suit her. "Thank you so much," she retorted. "Now that you know how I look, will you please leave? I have no intention of answering any questions, so—"

"Fire doesn't do a whole lot for your disposition, does it?" Alec interrupted. He shoved his hands into his pockets and took a couple of steps toward her. "As it happens, I wasn't planning on asking a whole lot of questions. I already spoke with the fire officials and the police. I know what happened."

"I doubt that," Christine muttered. She knew the official verdict on the fire, and she didn't agree with it.

"I also know you told the police the fire wasn't an accident."

Christine tightened her lips. "It wasn't."

Alec sighed, then spoke in a voice so reasonable it set her teeth on edge. "Now, Chrissy, I know you're upset, but let's not overreact here. I—"

"Overreact?" Christine was immensely insulted by that. "How do you overreact to someone trying to kill you for the fourth time?"

"No one is—"

"Yes, they are!" Christine slid off the table. "That fire was no accident. It's just too much of a coincidence that it happened right after your column came out."

"My column?" Alec's lips moved into a faint half smile. "My column didn't have anything to do—"

Was she the only person on the planet who could put this together? "Of course it did. How else do you think they found me?"

"They?"

"I don't know who *they* are!" Christine exclaimed, exasperated. "You don't get introduced to your killers before they try to kill you."

Alec grimaced and rubbed two fingers along his forehead. "You can't believe—"

"Of course that's what I believe!" Christine was suddenly furious with him. He was as responsible for that fire as the person who'd set it. "It is the only logical explanation! I was in that cottage for two days.

No one but my family knew I was there. Nothing happened. Then you told everyone in the world where to find me, and Keith's cottage burned to the ground. Do you really think that's just a coincidence?"

Alec's face seemed a shade paler. "Of course it's a coincidence! That fire did *not* happen because of something I wrote!"

"Yes, it did!" Christine drew in a shaky breath. "Actually, I guess I should be grateful to you. I was actually starting to think I *was* paranoid. Then you wrote your column, that fire happened and I know I'm not."

"My column had nothing—"

"It had everything to do with it!" She sighed heavily. "I suppose I shouldn't blame you for everything. After all, you can't help it if your readership includes potential murderers."

His head came up, his expression for once not showing any sign of amusement. He opened his mouth to speak, but his words were drowned out by a woman's voice. "Miss McKinley?"

Christine peered over Alec's wide shoulder. A uniformed nurse was standing just inside the door. "I can take you to your room now," she said. She looked from her to Alec, then back again. "Your visitor..."

"My visitor is leaving." Christine marched across the room. "He's got to get back to his office and write another story about me that will make me sound completely insane." She stopped in front of Alec. "Just don't go writing my obituary. I have every intention of living through this. I'm not going to let someone kill me without finding out who he is and why he wants to do it!"

Alec gave his head an impatient shake. "Come on, Chrissy, you don't—"

"Did I ever tell you that I really, really hate being called Chrissy?" Christine asked. "Well, I do. I also do *not* 'hock bean sprouts.' We don't even *sell* bean sprouts! And there isn't one thing wrong with my disposition. I'm a very even tempered person." She stalked to the door. "And I don't care if you like my knees or not!"

HE SHOULD HAVE STUCK with the blonde and the Mets game.

Alec drove too fast down the dark highway between Banff and Calgary, one hand on the steering wheel while the other clutched a cup of coffee. He'd already phoned in his story, and he hadn't made Christine sound completely insane. Actually, he hadn't mentioned one thing about their conversation, which in his estimation made him an extremely decent person.

So why did he feel like such a jerk?

Alec slowed the car to a stop at the side of the road and switched off the engine. He felt worse than a jerk.

He felt totally responsible for Chrissy's current predicament.

He pictured her in that hospital room, her face the color of the sheets, her gray eyes wide with shock. Damn, but she'd looked terrible. That wasn't surprising. He'd look just as bad if he thought someone was out to kill him.

That's what she thought, and she thought that because of what he'd written. He shouldn't have said anything about her location. If he'd given it more than a second's thought, he probably wouldn't have. However, he hadn't given it any thought at all. He'd dashed off the story about her the way he dashed off all his stories.

Now she was sitting in a hospital, believing that a crazed lunatic was out to get her. If he hadn't published her location, she'd probably believe the fire was simply an accident. She'd still be shocked, but she wouldn't be frightened.

That fear bothered him. It made him want to protect her, even though he knew there was nothing to protect her from. There was no crazed killer after her—at least, there better not be. If there was, Alec had unintentionally told said maniac where to find her.

He took a sip of his now-cold coffee and tried to reassure himself. There was no killer. Chrissy was just overreacting. Tomorrow she'd return to hocking yogurt and lima beans. Sooner or later she'd stop being paranoid, and she'd go on to lead a long and happy life as Ms. HoleSum Foods.

Either that or someone would find her and finish the job he'd tried to do tonight. Alec's body went cold at the thought. If that happened—if, by some fluke, angry Miss McKinley turned into dead Miss McKinley—Alec would have a hard time living with himself. He'd always feel like he'd flushed her out so a killer could take a stab at her.

He groaned out loud and let his head fall back against the headrest. The hell of it was he couldn't do anything to make it right. Christine didn't need a sportswriter. She needed someone to rescue her from her current situation. She needed a strong macho guy who would make her feel safe, so she could relax and get over this paranoia thing. She needed someone who could save her from a crazed killer if one showed up. Unfortunately, there didn't seem to be any rescuers applying for the position.

Unless he volunteered.

Alec almost spilled his coffee at that. He wasn't in the rescue business. He wrote a sports column, and directed killers to their victims.

He set the coffee cup down on the dashboard and drummed his fingers on the steering wheel. Actually, he wasn't a bad choice for the position of rescuer. Oh, he knew very little about dealing with paranoia and nothing about dealing with crazed killers, but apart from that, he was qualified. Paranoia had to be caused by stress, and the cure for that had to be relaxation. Alec was great at relaxing. As for a crazed killer, he didn't really think one existed. Even if one did, he wouldn't look anywhere near Alec for Chrissy.

The more he thought about it, the better the idea seemed. He could take a few days off work and hide her someplace safe, quiet and secluded. He could make her feel protected. And while he was doing that, he could check into this killer theory of hers. After all, he was a trained journalist. Harper was always after him to dig for a story. Well, this was a good opportunity to do that. Given a few days, a phone and his portable computer, he could find out everything there was to know about Christine McKinley. He could prove to both her and himself that no killer existed. Then she'd stop being paranoid, and he'd stop feeling like the favored candidate for the Creep of the Year award.

It seemed like the best solution for both of them. Of course, there was a strong possibility that Chrissy wouldn't care for the idea. She wasn't exactly a card-carrying member of the Alec O'Brian fan club. She might not leap at the suggestion that they spend the next few days alone together.

Alec started the car. Christine would have to adjust, because he'd made up his mind.

He was going to rescue her.

CHRISTINE OPENED her eyes, then closed them again. Either she was having a very bad dream or Alec O'Brian was lounging in the chair on the other side of the room.

She cautiously raised one eyelid and hoped for the best.

Alec met her gaze and grinned. "Oh, good," he said. "You're finally awake." He yawned and stretched. "It's about time. The sun is shining and the birds are singing, both of which are extremely annoying even without a hangover." He eased himself out of the chair. "So is the hospital staff, by the way. You would not believe how hard it was to sneak in here."

Christine opened both her eyes. Apparently it wasn't a bad dream. Alec was here, he looked more rumpled and wrinkled than usual and he was acting as if he had every right to be in her room.

She sat up so fast the motion made her dizzy. "Go away!" she exclaimed. "You get out of this room right this minute or—"

Alec tut-tutted. "You really have to work on that disposition thing. I think it's getting worse—or are you always crabby when you wake up?"

"No, I..." Christine lay back down. "I am never crabby—except when I see you, which is something I hope not to do again." She closed her eyes. "Goodbye."

There were a few moments of silence. Christine took a peek from under the cover of her lashes. Alec was standing right beside the bed, staring down at her.

She opened her eyes wide and sighed. "You are wasting your time. I am not, repeat not, going to tell you anything, so—"

"I'm not asking anything." He dragged the chair to the side of the bed and sat down, with his face a few inches above her own. "I'm not here to interview you. I'm here to rescue you."

"Rescue me?" Christine pulled the covers over her face. "I don't need to be rescued—certainly not by you. Go away."

He didn't. He kept talking. "Unfortunately, I don't think you have much choice. You have a problem."

"I certainly do," Christine mumbled. She pulled back the covers. "It's..." she peered at the red digits on the clock beside the bed "...seven a.m. There is a man in my room who I can't stand at the best of times, much less first thing in the morning. He doesn't seem to be going away, and any minute I am going to start screaming."

Alec patted her shoulder. "That's not a good idea. You don't look your best right now, and I'm sure you don't want two or three dozen reporters joining you for breakfast."

Christine stared numbly up at him. "They're still here?"

"Camped in the lobby." He sounded quite cheerful about it. "That's part of your problem. You're big news now. There aren't many places you can go and remain anonymous. Last week there were, but after last night…" He shook his head.

Christine wasn't ready to face this depressing news so early in the morning. "I'll figure something out."

Alec raised an eyebrow, wrinkling half of his forehead. "Like what? Your place in Florida? That will remain a secret for, oh, about eight minutes."

Christine had been awake half the night reviewing her options. Apart from locking herself in her condo and hiring two million security guards, she hadn't come up with much.

Alec continued. "And if reporters can find you, so can potential murderers—assuming they exist, of course."

"Of course," Christine retorted dryly. "But I don't have to worry about that, do I? I'm just a little neurotic, right?"

"I don't know." Alec averted his face, but she could see his jaw tense. "However, I plan on finding out."

What had they given her last night? She'd thought they were sleeping pills. Maybe they were a hallucinatory drug. "What was that?"

"I'm going to find out." Alec looked her full in the face. "At least, I'm going to try. And there's a good chance I'll succeed. I've got a lot of contacts, and access to a lot of information. Plus I know how to go about digging for a story. I might not do it much but that doesn't mean I don't know how. If someone has a motive for wanting you in a galaxy far, far away, I'm going to find it."

Now she knew she was hallucinating. "Why would you do that? You don't believe..."

"I do have my doubts." Alec scrubbed a hand down his face. "There isn't a whole lot of evidence to substantiate your theory. Even that thing last night—"

"Was just another accident," Christine said, completing his thought. "And I'm crazy." She eyed him suspiciously. "Is that what you're trying to do? Find conclusive evidence that I'm off my rocker?"

His lips twitched, showing his dimples. "Sort of."

"Be my guest." Christine closed her eyes. "Be sure to let me know when you've figured it out. That could be difficult, though, because as soon as you leave, which better happen in the next ten seconds, I don't plan on ever seeing you again."

"You'll see me, all right. You're coming with me."

Christine opened her eyes. He did look serious. "I'm not going anywhere with you."

"You have to. I'm rescuing you, remember? One of the requirements of a rescue is that the rescuer and the rescuee escape together." He leaned closer. "Now, here's the plan. You'll make a brief statement to the press, saying you're all right and you're going back to Calgary. 'Thank you all so much for your concern, you've got a wonderful fire department, terrific police, and the folks at the hospital have been abso-

lutely inspiring. Of course that fire was an accident—
I was in shock when I suggested otherwise.' You
come back inside, slip out through the staff door and
into my car. We leave before anyone figures it out. No
one will ever suspect you're with me."

"That's because I won't be," Christine muttered.

Alec ignored her. "I've got this place lined up. It's
in the foothills, it's quiet and secluded and only a
handful of people even know it exists. You'll get as
much peace and quiet as you want. That should make
a tremendous improvement in your disposition."

Christine tried to muster up a glare, but couldn't
because it sounded perfect. She chewed on her bottom lip, astonished with herself for even considering
it. "What's the catch?"

"There isn't one...except that I'll be there, too."

"Just you and me alone together?" That would definitely drive her over the edge. "No, thanks."

Alec's eyes sparkled with amusement. "What's the
problem? Are you afraid I'll ravish you or something?"

That thought hadn't even occurred to her. "No,
I..."

"Good, because I won't." He patted her shoulder.
"I don't have any designs on your bod. I'm just trying
to help you."

"Why would you help me?" Christine demanded.
"There are plenty of other sports figures around. If
you're dying to help someone, why not one of them?"

Alec winced and looked down at his fingers. "Because if something happens to one of them, I won't feel..." he cleared his throat "...responsible."

Had she heard that right? "What?"

"Responsible," Alec repeated. He glanced at her, then returned to studying his hands. "I'm not saying I did anything wrong. I was just doing my job. You're news. I found you, I talked to you and I wrote about it. That's what I do. I'm a reporter."

So much for her theory that he was a punishment from God. "All right," Christine agreed. "That's what a reporter does."

"But I did mention your location." He frowned at his right thumbnail. "There was nothing wrong with doing that. However, since I did, I, uh, feel slightly responsible for your current situation."

"You should," she agreed bitterly. He flinched, and Christine felt like a real bitch. Obviously something she'd said last night had hit home, and he was feeling badly about it—or as badly as he could feel about something. It did serve him right, but that didn't mean he was responsible for her. "It doesn't really matter," she said, around a long sigh. "They would have found me sooner or later."

"If there is a they." His head came up to its usual arrogant angle. "I'm not convinced there is." He looked sideways at her. "You've got to admit it's pretty far-fetched."

Christine stopped feeling sorry for him. He obviously didn't feel as badly as he should. "All right," she agreed. "It's far-fetched. I'm paranoid." She turned over on her side, with her back to him. "Case closed. Goodbye."

Alec put a hand on her shoulder and tugged her over onto her back. "The case isn't closed. You are going to come with me. You are going to rest and relax, while I find out if there's any chance someone could be after you."

Christine eyed him suspiciously. "And if there is?"

"I'll have enough evidence to take to the police." He flashed a far-too-charming smile. "And I'll write one hell of a story."

"Otherwise, you'll write that I'm crazy?" Christine guessed.

Alec hesitated. "Otherwise, I won't write anything."

Right. And if she believed that, she was an even bigger fool than he'd say she was in his column. However, perhaps it was worth the risk. Alec could have the skills and resources needed to find out who was after her. Certainly he would be a lot better at it than she would be. She didn't have a clue how to start.

It was tempting—except for the fact that he'd be around. Actually, even his presence might be better than being alone or surrounded by a bunch of low-brow armed guards. However... "I'm not the safest person to be with these days," she argued. "I know you don't believe that, but it's true."

Alec's mouth moved into a wicked grin. "Don't worry about it, baby," he said in a growly gangster voice. "I can handle the bad guys."

No, he couldn't. However, Christine wouldn't really need him to do that. If she and Alec were hidden away, it shouldn't be necessary. Still... "I don't know."

"What else can you do?" Alec asked. "Hide in Florida all alone? You'll end up talking to your alfalfa sprouts."

It was a good point. Christine squirmed uncomfortably as he continued. "Besides, you must want this settled. You make a lot of public appearances. Wouldn't you like to walk out in front of a crowd without worrying that some asshole is going to take another shot at you?"

"Of course, but..."

His grin was pure triumph. "Then come with me. Not only will I make sure you're safe, I'll do a thorough check into this and find out if something really is going on. If I don't find anything, you'll be able to stop worrying about it, and I'll be able to stop feeling responsible for you."

Christine gnawed on her bottom lip. "Well, um..."

"Good." Alec eased himself to his feet and pulled a folded piece of paper out of the inside pocket of his jacket. "Here's your press statement."

"My what?"

"Your press statement," Alec repeated, shoving the paper into her hand. "Read it and put on one of those shaken-but-bearing-up-bravely smiles. Oh, and be sure to show a little cleavage. That's all some of those guys came to see." He glanced around the room. "What's your clothing situation? Are those duds you had on yesterday all you managed to salvage from that fire?"

Christine nodded wordlessly.

"What size do you wear?"

"Eight, but..."

"Okay. I'll pick up some sensible-looking clothes for you and a few groceries. I'll meet you outside the staff entrance right after the press conference."

"But—"

"If you're not there, I'll have to come in after you and carry you out over my shoulder." He eyed her as if assessing her weight. "That might not be a bad idea. I think most rescues do begin that way."

He actually seemed rather taken with the idea. Christine felt a surge of panic. "You're not carrying me anywhere. And I haven't agreed—"

"Too late." He opened the door and flashed a roguish, piratical smile. "This rescue has officially started."

4

ALEC WAS RIGHT about one thing. She was big news now.

Christine watched an early morning talk show on the television in her room while she dressed. The laundry staff had washed her clothes, and the nurses had even supplied a small selection of cosmetics. Even with their help, she couldn't disguise the paleness of her face or the shocked look in her eyes. Still, once she was showered and dressed, she felt much more capable of coping with the world.

Alone.

Alec's offer to rescue her was very nice—if she could trust him, which she most certainly couldn't. He was either digging for a story or, at the very least, trying to appease a slightly guilty conscience. Either way, she wasn't going to go along with it. There were other solutions to her problem besides spending a few days alone with a man who thought she was crazy—especially when that man was Alec O'Brian.

She was sitting in the chair Alec had vacated, trying not to think about his good-looking face, when her own face flashed across the television. "And in other news, former golfing star Christine McKinley narrowly escaped death last night when the cottage she was staying in exploded in a mass of flames." They switched to a tape of the fire, zooming in on her, a blanket around her shoulders, being led into an ambulance. "According to Banff medical staff, Ms. McKinley was not injured, although she remained in the Banff hospital overnight."

The scene changed to the front of the hospital. The announcer went into a brief description of her golfing career, ending with the taped scene of her announcing her retirement, a little blurb about HoleSum Foods and the information that the fire was nothing more than an accident. "A spokesperson for HoleSum Foods denies rumors that Ms. McKinley believes her life is in danger." The picture flashed to a serious-looking young man Christine recognized as a member of the public-relations department. "Naturally, Ms. McKinley was shaken by the incident, but she is in good spirits and will be attending the opening of the HoleSum Foods store in Chicago next week."

"Good spirits?" Christine echoed. She stared at the screen as the announcer went on with another story. "Someone is trying to kill me, but I'm in good spirits?" She gave the switch on the television a disgusted smack, then roamed restlessly around the room. She couldn't blame the HoleSum Foods people for saying she was "in good spirits," since that's what she'd told the company president when she'd spoken with him this morning. She hadn't been able to think of anything else to say. If she'd told Mr. Kleinghammer that she thought her life was in danger, he might have immediately canceled her contract. It wasn't that he was an unfeeling man, but it did sound far-fetched, and he did have HoleSum's image to consider.

She wandered over to the window and took a look outside. The parking lot was full of cars, and there was a news team filming the hospital. "Wonderful," Christine complained. "Eight years on the professional-golf circuit, two as the HoleSum Foods lady, and what am I most famous for? Almost getting blown up!"

When she found herself hoping for an earthquake to occur in another part of the world, she dropped the blinds and stepped back. This was even worse than she'd thought. Not only was she news here in Alberta, but that program she'd been watching was seen all over the continent.

Not that it mattered much. Her face was on boxes of granola, cans of real-fruit compote and a wide variety of vitamin supplements. Only a nutritionally challenged person who didn't own a television and didn't read a newspaper would fail to recognize her. Hiding was almost an impossibility.

She sank into a chair, horrified by her predicament. Where was she going to go? Her place in Florida wasn't an option. She'd never feel safe there. Besides, there were other people living in nearby condos. She didn't want anything to happen to them! She could join her mother and brother in France but that wouldn't help, either. There was no guarantee that whoever was after her wouldn't follow her there—or be waiting for her when she got back.

Maybe there was no one. Maybe Estelle was right. Maybe this danger was all in her mind.

Christine looked down at her hands, frowning when she realized they were trembling a little. There had been four attempts on her life. She hadn't imagined any of them. She needed to go someplace quiet and safe, where she could figure out what was going on before it began affecting her career. A place she'd be so well hidden that she wouldn't be afraid. A place...exactly like Alec had described.

She glanced at the statement he had written. It was actually pretty good. He had offered to protect her—insisted on it, as a matter of fact. If she didn't show up, he might really come in here and carry her out over his shoulder. Christine giggled slightly at the thought, then immediately sobered.

The sad truth was that she didn't have many choices.

She was simply going to have to let Alec come to her rescue.

THIS RESCUE STUFF wasn't that difficult, Alec decided.

He steered the car down the highway, feeling

pleased with himself. He was positive that the most difficult part of this task was already over—and it had gone exactly as he'd planned. The press conference had run smoothly, although Chrissy hadn't done the cleavage bit he'd recommended. There had been a few tense moments while he'd waited for her to show up at the rendezvous point, but just when he'd decided he'd have to go in after her, she'd made an appearance, looking pale, uncertain and nervous.

She still looked that way. Alec glanced at her out of the corner of his eye. She had on the same outfit she'd been wearing last night—brown shorts and a green silk blouse. Her face was still too white, and her gray eyes still held some remnants of shock.

However, her knees were holding up quite nicely.

Alec jerked his attention back to the road. He had no illusions about why Chrissy was here. She hadn't suddenly decided that he was Mr. Wonderful. She simply hadn't been able to come up with any other options.

However, after a couple of days of resting and relaxing in his company, a lot of things could change.

Alec was ninety-nine percent convinced that getting Chrissy rested and relaxed was going to be the main focus of this mission. He'd had another talk with the fire officials this morning, and they'd assured him that the explosion was officially listed as an accident, caused by a faulty gas heater in the cottage.

He'd also spoken with other reporters attending the press conference. They, too, believed Chrissy's recent accidents were no more than that. All Alec had to do was produce a little proof and get Chrissy to relax enough to believe it.

And the sooner he got her to their destination, the sooner she could start relaxing. Alec took another look at her. She was sitting stiffly in the seat, her shoulders tense, her hands clasped tightly together in her lap. Her entire attention was focused on the rearview mirror outside her window.

He pressed harder on the gas pedal, a little surprised at how protective he felt toward her. When he was alone with a woman, protecting her was usually the last thing on his mind. However, right now all he wanted to do was put his arm around Christine and assure her that everything was going to be all right.

Given her temperamental disposition, that probably wasn't a good idea.

"A red Ford sedan, a green truck and a half-dozen white or off-white cars," he reported.

Christine swiveled her head to face him. "What?"

"That's what's behind us. They're all occupied by couples doing obscene things to one another, or families with far too many children. I don't think any of them are interested in us."

"I hope not," Christine muttered.

Alec tried again. "No one was around when you

got into my car. No one knows you're with me and no one knows where we're going."

"Neither do I," Christine complained. "Where exactly are we going?"

"Marty's place." Christine looked blank, so Alec explained, "That's my cousin. He inherited my aunt's farm a few years ago. Marty rents out the land but no one really lives in the house."

Christine's eyes grew round. "*You* have a cousin?"

"Dozens of them." He noted her surprised expression. "Why?"

"Well, um..." Her cheeks colored slightly. "You're not the sort of person people associate with, uh, relatives."

Alec chuckled at that. "I have tons of relatives. Us O'Brians are a prolific bunch." He took another look at her face. "What about you? Do you have lots of relatives?"

Christine shook her head. "Not here, no. Just my mother and my brother. My father passed away a few years ago. He didn't have much family. And my mother is from England, so all of her relatives are over there."

"Is that where she is now?"

"Partly." Christine glanced out the back window again. "Keith's in France...one of those see-Europe-in-six-weeks tours."

Alec considered that. It explained why she didn't have any family around to help her. However, he would have thought she had other men in her life to do it. Why didn't she?

He was reviewing the possibilities when Christine spoke again. "This cousin of yours, Marty—what exactly did you tell him? Does he know I'm..."

She didn't have much confidence in his abilities at subterfuge, did she? "I didn't tell him anything about you. This is a rescue mission, remember? Rescues are conducted in complete secrecy."

Christine didn't look too impressed by this. "Then what *did* you tell Marty?"

"He's a guy, Chrissy. I didn't have to tell him anything. I just asked him if I could use the place. He often lends it out, so he didn't ask any questions. He just said I could use it as long as I wanted, as long as I left it clean, picked up the beer cans and remembered to cut the grass." He executed a quick shoulder check before making a lane change. "Come to think of it, I believe cutting grass is one of the responsibilities of the rescuee."

"Is it?" Christine murmured vaguely. She took an anxious look out the back.

"Yes, it is." Alec was beginning to be a little irritated by her attitude. "And worrying about our safety isn't."

"What?"

"Worrying about our safety is not your responsibility." He took the Cremona exit ramp. "You don't know a whole lot about rescues, do you?"

Christine smiled faintly. "Well, I've never actually been rescued before, but…"

"I didn't think so. You don't seem to know any of the rules."

"Rules?"

"Uh-huh." Alec checked the merge lane and pulled onto the secondary highway. "There are rules for this sort of thing."

Her smile grew. "Oh, really?"

"Uh-huh. And one of those rules is that you are not allowed to worry about safety. That's my job. I do neat stuff like that and you don't. Got it?"

She focused on his face, her lips twitching upward. "What exactly am I supposed to do? Besides cutting the grass, I mean."

"Rest, relax, look helpless and tell me I'm wonderful," Alec responded promptly. He glanced sideways to check her expression. "You can start on the telling-me-I'm-wonderful part anytime now."

Christine blinked a couple of times. Then she rested her head back against the seat and laughed out loud.

Alec grinned as well. Her humor wasn't particularly appropriate, but that smile was just as appealing as her knees.

ALEC MIGHT BE AMUSING, but Christine was still wondering about the wisdom of her actions when they arrived at their destination.

It wasn't that there was anything wrong with the house. Actually, it was the perfect place to hide out for a few days.

It was a small, two-story farmhouse, located at the end of a narrow gravel road and set back a good half mile from the main highway. It was almost completely surrounded by trees, keeping it and its occupants well hidden from view. The grass at the front needed cutting, but apart from that the place seemed well maintained.

The inside was the same. Christine wandered through the three upstairs bedrooms, noting that although the place could have used a good dusting, it was tidy. Her estimation of the anonymous Marty and his equally anonymous friends was high, but then plummeted when she found a half-empty box of condoms in the bathroom cupboard. Apparently Marty's friends did more than cut the grass when they came here.

She gave the cupboard door a hasty shove and took the stairs down to the main level, which consisted of a living room, dining room and sunny country kitchen. The whole place was furnished with odd pieces of mismatched furniture that had obviously been chosen for comfort rather than style. There were rag rugs on the floor of the living room, and the walls were papered with old-fashioned, faded wallpaper. The few modern conveniences—a television, VCR and satellite receiver in the living room, and the microwave on the kitchen counter—looked slightly out of place.

Christine stopped in the kitchen doorway and watched Alec pile plastic grocery bags on the gray-and-white counter. "That's everything," he announced.

"It certainly looks like everything," Christine agreed. She eyed the mountain of bags on the counter. Either Alec was a really big eater or he'd planned on hiding out for a couple of decades. "How much do you eat?"

"It's not all for me. I had to get a large selection. Healthy stuff for you, and some decent food for me." He peeled off his jacket and tossed it over the back of a wooden kitchen chair. "Rescuers are real men. Real men don't eat a lot of health food."

"Oh?" Christine peered into a bag containing a bag of Cheezies, another of pretzels and three kinds of potato chips. "In that case, I'd say real men have a very short life expectancy."

Alec chuckled, but Christine immediately regretted the comment. It reminded her of her own life expectancy, which right now didn't seem too promising.

She watched Alec pull a few items out of a grocery bag and felt a sudden burst of unease. Alec was far too casual about this. He obviously didn't understand that they could be in danger. That was because he thought the danger was all in her head.

Christine glanced around the room and sighed.

This place seemed safe enough. On the other hand, so had Keith's cabin, and look what had happened to it. She didn't want another structure she didn't own to burn to the ground, and she didn't want to put anyone else in danger, either.

And, she had to admit, the situation was a little disconcerting. She hadn't had a roommate since she'd left home, and she'd never lived with a man before. Now she was all alone in the middle of nowhere with one—and a very good-looking one at that.

It wasn't his charms that had her concerned, Christine reminded herself. She was quite capable of resisting those. Still, it might be best if she left here—for a variety of reasons.

She watched Alec turn to open a cupboard and took a deep breath. "Listen, I'm, uh, not so sure this is a good idea."

"What's not a good idea?" He began setting cans in the cupboard. "Not eating the same food? Don't worry about it. If I find your healthy ways getting to me, I can always tie you down and force-feed you junk food." He glanced at her over his shoulder and winked. "Actually, that might be fun."

An unwanted mental image of him doing just that flashed through Christine's mind. She shoved it impatiently aside. "I wasn't talking about food. I was talking about this, uh, arrangement."

"What about it?"

"It's not a good idea," Christine explained to his

back. "I mean, uh, the last place I was in blew up. I don't think Marty would appreciate that happening to his house."

"He didn't mention it." Alec set a box on the middle shelf. "He just told me to leave the place clean and cut the grass. He didn't say anything about not blowing it up."

Was it possible to have a serious discussion with this man? "Alec!"

"Nothing is going to blow up, Chrissy." Alec performed a slow-motion pivot to face her. "This is our secret hideaway—and it really is a secret. No one knows you're here."

"Someone could find out." She sighed at the skepticism on his face. "I know you don't believe..."

"That's what I'm going to find out. If there is a someone."

"Are you really going to do that?"

"Uh-huh." His lips curled upward. "It's what I'm going to be doing while you rest, relax, look helpless and tell me I'm wonderful."

Right. And given his obvious disbelief, the possibility of him actually doing something was zero to none. "Still, I don't think I should stay here. I—"

"You have to stay here. The rescuee and the rescuer have to stay together. It's another rule."

"Maybe it is, but..."

"And another rule is that the rescuee can't change her mind." He set a bag of dried fruit down on the counter, leaned back and folded his arms. "You can't have the dashing hero saving a damsel in distress, at severe risk to his own body, only to have her decide she didn't mind being in distress!" He shook his head. "That's not how it works. A rescue isn't over until the rescuer says it's over. That means I get to decide when this rescue is finished. You have no say in the matter."

"Oh, for heaven sakes!" Christine exclaimed. "Will you stop making up rules and listen to me? I'm not sure it's safe—"

He aimed a finger at her. "That's something else you're not allowed to do. You are not allowed to worry about safety. Have you forgotten already? That was the first rule."

Christine was getting a little tired of him and his rules. "I thought the first rule was that I had to cut the grass. And—"

"No, it isn't. Cutting the grass is one of the duties of the rescuee. It's not a rule. Not worrying about our safety is a rule and you just broke it."

"I don't care. I—"

His eyebrows rose steeply. "You should care. There are severe penalties associated with breaking the rules." He unfolded his arms. "And the penalty for breaking that one is that *you* have to put away all the groceries."

Christine stared at him, startled by the sudden change in conversation. "What?"

"Actually, you should be the one to put this stuff away anyway. That way you'll be able to find things when you're cooking."

"Cooking?" Christine repeated. How had cooking got into this conversation?

"Uh-huh. One of the duties of a rescuee is to cook great meals." He picked up his brown briefcase and meandered across the room toward the hall. "You might as well get busy on that now, while I attend to more serious business." He gave her shoulder a bracing pat as he passed. "Oh, and you should start practicing telling me I'm wonderful. You're not very good at it."

Christine opened her mouth to give him her opinion of that, but before she could formulate the words, he'd left the room.

She glared at the empty doorway for a moment, then turned to the pile of grocery bags. "Some rescue this is turning out to be," she complained. "I mow the lawn. I cook the meals. Apparently the only things I don't do are worry about safety and decide when the whole farce is over. Seems the most important things now are being handled by Mr. Alec O'Brian."

She giggled a little hysterically and began pulling out cans of food. She might as well stay here, for a few days anyway. She didn't seem to have much choice, since Alec had the keys to the only transportation around. Besides, this place was probably as safe as anywhere else, and she should have some warning if trouble did arrive. And maybe, just maybe, Alec would stumble across something that would be useful—when he wasn't making up ridiculous rules, that is.

She pulled out a package of jumbo ballpark franks, barbecue sauce included, and wrinkled her nose.

However, if he was expecting her to cook this stuff, he was in for a big disappointment.

5

ACTUALLY, Alec didn't complain too much about the meal she put together.

He ate an enormous plate of spaghetti, which he smothered in sauce, but barely touched his salad. "It's too green," he explained as he dried a plate. "Real men don't eat a lot of green food."

"They should." Christine rinsed the spaghetti pot and set it on the draining board. "Lettuce is a good source of fiber."

"So is tree bark, but you don't see a lot of people eating that." He paused in the midst of putting away the plate to eye her warily. "You aren't going to try to push a lot of healthy stuff on me, are you?"

"Of course. If I have to do all the cooking, that's all you'll get." She drained the water from the sink. "I have a lovely lima-bean-and-broccoli casserole planned for tomorrow."

Alec shuddered dramatically. "Don't you dare," he warned. "There are severe penalties for serving lima beans during a rescue. Besides, I don't believe lima beans are food. I suspect they're really visitors from

outer space, and that eating them constitutes a decla-
ration of war against Alpha Centurius 3."

Christine struggled not to smile. This was a serious
situation, and Alec spent far too much time joking
around. She didn't want to encourage him. "Nonsense!"

"You won't think it's nonsense if the world is an-
nihilated by vegetables carrying leafy green fiber
guns." He put the plates in a cupboard and frowned
over at her. "You know, Chrissy, when I said you had
to put away the groceries, I didn't mean you had to
disinfect the entire kitchen."

"I couldn't possibly put food in those cupboards
without disinfecting them. And that fridge..." Christine shuddered. "Next time you're talking to Marty
tell him to put 'clean the fridge' on the list of things
people have to do before they leave this place."

In truth, neither the cupboards nor the fridge had
been in bad shape. However, Christine had rather enjoyed cleaning them out. Organizing the food had
made her feel as if she was in control of something,
even if it was just the canned spaghetti sauce. She'd
also enjoyed planning and cooking the meal. She very
seldom had the chance to cook for herself these days,
much less someone else.

She watched Alec dry the rest of the dishes, admir-
ing the lazy grace of his motions. So far it hadn't been
too bad having him around. He might not be her first
choice for a roommate, but there was something com-

forting about hearing him rattle around in the dining room, or having him wander into the kitchen in search of food. His nonchalant attitude had gone a long way toward restoring her equilibrium. It was almost impossible to remain tense while he was making jokes about rescues or teasing her about her choice of food.

She realized she was staring and turned back to the sink. She was not here to be distracted from the situation, she reminded herself. She was here so they could find out who was after her. So far Alec hadn't done much of that. "When does this investigative stuff start to happen?" she asked. "All I've seen you do is set your computer on the dining-room table."

"That is now officially my office," Alec informed her. "And I happened to be performing one of the most important steps in a rescue. The setup."

"That took all afternoon?" Christine shook her head. At this rate it would take a year and a half for him to get around to actually accomplishing something—assuming he really was going to do some investigating. She took a deep breath and dried her hands on the towel he'd tossed on the counter. "Well, now that you've done that, you must be ready to go on to the next step—finding out who is after me."

"Oh, is that the next step?" Alec took a corner of the towel she was holding to wipe his hands. "I thought the next step might be wrestling a grizzly or something. Rescuers are always doing stuff like that."

His fingers bumped against hers as he used the towel. It was the lightest of touches, but it took Christine's mind completely off the conversation. She cleared her throat and spoke in a brisk, no-nonsense tone. "There aren't any grizzlies after me. However, someone out there is." She jerked her thumb toward the door.

Alec rested his back against the counter, shoved his hands into his pants pockets and tilted his head to one side to study her. "You really believe that?"

Was he going to start that again? "Yes, I do."

"Why?"

"Why?" Christine echoed. She dropped the dish towel onto the counter and faced him. "I was almost run down in a parking lot, and I did *not* imagine it. Someone nearly attacked me in my condo, and I did *not* imagine that, either. Then someone fired a gun in my presence, and after that, the house I was staying in blew up! Either somebody is out to get me or four somebodies are out to get me. But I don't think I've suddenly become accident prone!" She took a breath. "Now, you said you'd help me find out what's going on. If you're not going to do that, I—"

Alec whistled softly between his teeth. "I don't think you should clean any more cupboards. It doesn't do one thing for your disposition."

"*My* disposition—"

"Is incredibly touchy. Yes, I know." His lips twitched with a smile. "Don't get your buns in a knot,

Chrissy. I'm going to do what I said I'd do. I was just seeing what your views were on the subject."

"My views haven't changed since last night. Someone is trying to kill me! I have to find out who."

"That's what I'm going to do. Villain identification. It's an important part of every rescue." He straightened in his distracting, muscle-by-muscle manner. "And it just so happens that while I was performing the exhausting job of setting up, I was also formulating a plan."

Christine found that hard to believe. "You were?"

"Uh-huh." He made a bowing, sweeping motion with one hand. "If you will step into my office, I will explain it to you."

Christine led the way into the dining room. His portable computer was set up on the table, with a number of cords running into the wall socket. The telephone was beside the computer, and there was an open notebook in front of that. Christine was mildly impressed. It did look as if he was planning on doing something.

He ushered her into an ancient oak and green leather chair, took a seat at the end of the table and picked up his notebook. "Motive, means and opportunity," he read from it. "That's what you need for a crime to take place." He glanced up, grinning. "I saw that on a detective show." He returned to his notes. "Unfortunately, almost everyone has the means, since it isn't too difficult to drive a car, break into an apartment, get a gun or blow up something. As for the opportunity, well, it's not that hard to find you. All you have to do is follow the trail of bean sprouts, and sooner or later they'll lead to you."

"I already figured that out for myself," Christine complained. "And—"

"I believe your line is, 'Brilliant deduction, Alec,'" he interjected. "The rescuee is supposed to tell the rescuer he's brilliant at least once a day." He consulted his notebook again. "Now, as I was saying, since means and opportunity don't help us, I have concluded that we should start with the motive. We need—"

"But I can't think of anyone with a motive! I tried before and..."

Alec gave her a look of utter disgust and tossed his notebook onto the table. "It is against the rules to interrupt the rescuer when he's explaining his plan." He folded his arms. "And the penalty for doing it..."

Christine didn't want him to go into another monologue about rescue rules and penalties! "All right," she said quickly. "I apologize for interrupting, and I'm amazed at the brilliance of your deductions. Do go on."

"Thank you." He flashed a smug smile before picking up his notebook. "Where was I? Oh yes, the motive. We need to find someone who has one." He raised an inquiring eyebrow. "You say you can't think of anyone?"

"No, I can't." Christine bent her head and stroked a couple of fingers across her forehead. It was almost impossible to believe that someone she knew wanted to kill her. However, there just wasn't any other explanation for what had been happening. "But there must be someone," she insisted. She looked up at Alec. "I know you don't believe—"

"I'm a trained journalist, Chrissy. I'm quite capable of keeping an open mind on the subject. If there's someone out there with a motive for doing you in, I'm going to find him."

Christine studied his features. He did seem sincere. She desperately wanted to believe that he was. "How are you going to do that?"

"Well..." He leaned back in his chair and tapped a pencil thoughtfully against his bottom lip. "I think the best way to approach this is as if I'm doing an in-depth article about you. For one thing, that's what I told my boss I was going to do, so if anyone phones the paper and asks, they'll confirm it. For another, it's a good cover story. I can talk to everyone without letting them know what I'm really after."

It did sound good. Christine's estimation of Alec rose. "Who will you talk to?"

"Everyone who has ever had anything to do with you. Your family. The people at HoleSum Foods. The women you used to golf with. Sportswriters who cover the tour." He flashed a smile. "I worked for a sports magazine before I took the job with the *Centen-*

nial, so I know most of them. They're a good source of information." He continued explaining, "People have a tendency to talk a lot to reporters. They probably won't announce they're trying to do you in, but they won't be singing your praises, either." He looked her straight in the eye. "If I do all that, and I come up with nothing, will you be satisfied that you're in no danger?"

Christine considered it for a moment. It wasn't a bad plan, assuming he'd really carry through with it. "Yes," she said. "Yes, I will."

"Good." He picked up his pen. "Let's start at the beginning. Where were you born and who was present at the time?"

"ONE THING is for certain," Alec announced an hour or so later. "The airlines don't make my suspect list." He eyed her with outright astonishment. "Twenty-three cities in fifty-two weeks? Don't you do anything but work?"

"Of course I do. I—"

"When?" Alec demanded. He referred to his notebook. "Just listen to your life. You spent most of your youth preparing for a golfing career. You spent eight years on the tour, playing in practically every tournament there was. Even in the off-season you spent most of your time practicing! You left that and started at HoleSum. Now you rush around from city to city, with hardly a break in between."

"There are lots of breaks in between," Christine objected. "And—"

"Yeah, and what do you do during them? Review marketing reports. Organize more charity affairs. Hunt around for sponsors so inner-city kids can play sports. And practice, practice, practice!" He shook his head. "This isn't my idea of retirement."

What did he expect her to do—take up knitting? "I was only twenty-eight when I retired. It's a little young for a nursing home."

"Couldn't you have found something less stressful than this?"

Christine's jaw started to ache. "I wasn't looking for something less stressful! I didn't retire because of my nerves, Alec, no matter what anyone says."

"No?" His forehead furrowed. "Why did you retire then?"

"Well... " Christine struggled for the words to explain. "There were a lot of reasons, I suppose. For one thing, my father died. He'd always been my biggest fan. He was the one who came to watch. My brother is quite a bit older than me, and he's busy with his own career. And my mother didn't really understand how anyone could golf for a living. But Dad, he loved it." She rested her head back and stared off into the distance, remembering. "When he wasn't around anymore, I sort of...lost interest in it. And, as you so unkindly pointed out the other day, I wasn't playing very well. I didn't want to be mediocre at it. If I couldn't put my heart and soul into it, I didn't want to do it at all.''

"You can put your heart and soul into health food?''

Christine heard the teasing note in his voice and straightened. "It isn't just the health food. Oh, I like the products well enough, but that's not why I'm doing it. It's all the other things. Setting up the sports programs for the inner-city children, working with the communities, finding sponsors....''

Alec rolled his eyes toward the ceiling. "There must be some way you can do that without working a million hours a day.''

Christine compressed her lips. He was voicing something she'd found herself wondering about more than once recently. "That's not important right now,'' she reminded both of them. "The important thing is to find out who is trying to kill me so I can get back to doing my job.''

Alec patted her knee. "Don't worry about it. I'll have this settled in a few days.''

Christine highly doubted that. He didn't believe there was anything to settle—and after a couple of hours of being interrogated by him, she couldn't blame him.

She gestured toward his notebook. "It's not much of a suspect list, is it?''

"There are some possibilities,'' Alec admitted.

"Both your mother and your brother stand to inherit a fair chunk of change if something happens to you."

Goose bumps rose on Christine's arms. She rarely thought about things like that, but now that he'd mentioned it...

She shoved the suspicion aside, ashamed of herself for even thinking it. "My mother wouldn't hurt me and neither would Keith. And I'm sure neither of them needs my money. My father left my mother very well-off, and Keith doesn't care about stuff like that. All he's interested in is touring castles."

At least, that's all he'd ever talked about to her. Christine bit on her lip as she considered it. She really didn't know Keith very well. He was eight years older than she was, and they'd never had a lot in common. They got together a few times a year, but they didn't share confidences. "Besides, he's in Europe right now," she added. "I think that eliminates him."

"It probably does, but I'll check into him, anyway." Alec raised a hand to massage the back of his neck. "Then there's HoleSum's competition. They might benefit if you weren't around. Or it could be that one of your former competitors is holding a grudge against you."

He sounded pretty doubtful, and that was how Christine felt. None of those seemed like good reasons for someone to go to all the trouble of bumping her off.

Alec stretched his back and rotated his shoulders before reexamining his notes. "What about friends? You've only mentioned your former caddie, and a few women on the tour. Is there anyone else?"

Christine bit her lip. There was one name she hadn't mentioned. She hadn't told Alec anything about Estelle—and she didn't think she should. Estelle was a good friend, but she did have a tendency to go on and on about this compulsive-memory thing. Christine didn't think Alec needed to hear that. "No," she said firmly. "That's everybody."

"You're sure?"

Christine nodded. Alec studied her face for a moment, then shrugged. "Okay." He glanced down at his notebook, then back at her. "What about men? You must have been through a fair number of those. Have you left any broken hearts behind, run off with someone's husband for a hot weekend or...?"

Christine flushed and shook her head. "Oh no. Nothing like that."

Alec's eyes gleamed with curiosity. "I should check them out, anyway."

Christine squirmed uncomfortably. Her limited experience in this area hadn't bothered her before. However, she had no desire to share the details with Alec. "There really isn't anything to check out."

Alec held up a hand. "It's my job to decide that."

"It's not—"

"The rescuer has to know everything there is to

know about the person he's protecting. It's one of the rules."

Christine studied his expression, then sighed and gave up. It was clear he wasn't going to drop this line of questioning until she told him something. "Oh, all right. There was Jeffrey Thurbern. He's a lawyer from Detroit. I was seeing him about four years ago. And last year there was an accountant...." She struggled for a name, embarrassed at how hard it was to remember. "Bruce Davidson. He lives in, um, Seattle."

Alec wrote that down, then looked expectantly at her. "Go on."

Christine shook her head. "There isn't anyone else."

"There must be someone more recent."

"There isn't," Christine insisted. "Oh, I've had dinner with a few men, but I haven't been involved in a relationship since...well, since Bruce, I guess."

"But that was a year ago." Alec's eyes widened. "Are you telling me that you haven't been with a man for over a year?"

"No, I haven't," she confirmed, refusing to feel embarrassed. She took in his expression of utter disbelief and frowned. "It's difficult to establish relationships with my schedule. Besides..."

"Not that difficult!" He shoved his fingers through his hair in a gesture of exasperation. "Geez, Chrissy, I have at least one 'relationship' a week—and that's a slow week!"

Christine glowered at him. "My idea of a relationship is not one that lasts two hours!"

"Why not?" His voice lowered to a sexy drawl. "It's a great two hours."

Christine's body thudded into awareness at his tone. There wasn't a doubt in her mind that this was one thing Alec was very good at doing. "I don't do things that way," she said stiffly. "I—"

"It sounds to me as if you don't do it at all." His eyes searched her face, his expression that of quizzical astonishment. "Why is that? Don't you like it?"

Actually, Christine couldn't ever recall being overwhelmed by the experience. "That has nothing to do with it! I have to be emotionally involved with someone before I get physically involved. That means I have to spend a lot of time with him, get to know him—and that's difficult with my schedule. Besides, I'm busy with other things, and I don't consider that a priority."

"You don't consider *that* a priority?" Alec echoed. He peered at her from under lowered eyebrows. "If you don't consider *that* a priority, what do you consider a priority?"

"Well, my job and..."

"Your job?" His voice rose, his tone incredulous. "You think hocking bean sprouts is more important than sex?"

"I do *not* hock bean sprouts!" Christine snapped. "And my sex life..."

"Once a year does not constitute a sex life!"

Then once a decade was probably out as well. "All right," Christine conceded. "But my lack of a sex life doesn't have anything to do with finding out who is trying to kill me." She bounced out of the chair. "And I really wish you'd stop acting as if there is something wrong with me."

Alec followed her movements with a speculative gaze. "Is there something wrong with you?"

Christine's jaw started aching again. "No, there—"

"Never mind," Alec interrupted. His chair squeaked across the floorboards as he pushed it back from the table. "I'd rather find out for myself."

Christine watched uneasily as he got to his feet. "What does...?"

"I just don't think I should take your word for it." He slid an arm around her waist and pulled her to him. "Besides, I'm really curious now."

Christine mumbled a protest that came a second too late. His hand closed around her chin, holding it firmly in place. Then he lowered his head and settled his lips over hers.

Christine stood perfectly still, stunned by a multitude of sensations. His hand against her back, so warm she could feel his fingers through her thin silk blouse. His scent filling her nostrils. His breath against her face. His body pressing hard against her own.

She made a small sound that was half objection,

half appreciation. Alec widened his stance, fitting her between his thighs. He slid his tongue across her bottom lip, then stroked it into her mouth, while the hand on her back caressed lower, urging her hips forward. It felt erotic and wicked and sinful and... absolutely wonderful.

Then Christine was struggling out of the embrace, mortified by her reaction. What was she doing? This was Alec O'Brian, for heaven sakes. She didn't even like him that much! She certainly shouldn't be kissing him.

She backed away from him, blinking to bring him back into focus. "What on earth do you think you're doing?"

"It's called kissing." His tone was husky and there was a reddish tinge on his cheekbones. "And I wasn't the only one doing it."

Christine's face heated to an unbearable warmth. "Well, we're not going to be doing any more of it! And if you've brought me here to get me into bed, I—"

Alec let out his breath with a puff. "Geez, Chrissy, if you overreact this bad when someone kisses you, it's no wonder you don't have a sex life!"

"I'm not overreacting!"

"Ah, you are so." He straightened and returned to his chair. "I don't have to rescue women to get them into bed. They usually just wander in there by themselves."

His easy manner made Christine feel gauche and ridiculous. He had a point. He probably didn't have to do much at all to get women to sleep with him. Still... "Then why did you...?"

"What? That kiss?" Alec made a dismissive gesture with a hand. "That was just research."

"Research?"

"Uh-huh." He opened his eyes in a wide, innocent expression. "Remember, the rescuer has to know everything there is to know about the person he's protecting. I was finding out if something was wrong with you." His lips moved into a slow, smug, self-satisfied smile as he surveyed her. "I'm pleased to report that there isn't."

MAYBE THERE WAS something wrong with her, Christine decided a few hours later. She'd actually liked kissing Alec O'Brian. Either she'd lost her marbles or she was coming down with a serious disease.

She sat up in bed and switched on the light. There was nothing wrong with her. It had been over a year since a man had kissed her, that's all. It was only natural that she was a little stimulated by the experience.

So why had she let it go on that long?

Christine climbed out of bed and paced to the window. It wasn't just lack of opportunity, she admitted to herself. She'd met a number of men. If she'd wanted a casual fling, she could have had one. However, casual flings weren't her style. She didn't believe in meaningless affairs between two people who didn't care about each other.

Yet she hadn't made any effort to establish any sort of meaningful relationship after her last one ended. There just didn't seem to be any point. With her schedule, it was much too difficult to have any sort of relationship. Besides, she hadn't considered it particularly important. There were lots of other things in her life that demanded her attention, and they'd all seemed more important than romance.

Perhaps that had been a mistake. Perhaps she should have devoted more time to her personal life. Maybe if she had, she would have someone around to help her who really cared about her. And maybe she wouldn't be all hot and bothered by one experimental kiss from a decidedly disreputable reporter.

"Oh, for heaven sakes!" Christine exclaimed. She returned to the bed and sat down on it. Just because she'd liked being kissed didn't mean she'd made any mistakes. Her life was perfectly fine the way it was. She didn't need a man in it right now. She was just feeling this way because it was the middle of the night, it was dark outside, the house creaked and she was a little nervous.

The house creaked again, and Christine rubbed her hands up and down her arms. Okay, she was a lot nervous. During the daylight, with Alec around to joke about the situation, she'd felt safe here. Now she didn't. Maybe someone had followed them here—or had somehow deduced where she was. Maybe the entire house was going to go up in flames, or some bozo was going to rush in here with a lethal weapon and...

She took a few deep breaths, gave her left thumb an experimental shake and studied it. She was firmly convinced that her twitching thumb meant she was in danger. How reliable a method was that, though? Would it always twitch? What if something happened in the middle of the night? Would a twitching thumb wake her up? If it did, what would she do? Rush into Alec's room and tell him she knew there was a problem because her thumb was twitching? That was hardly likely to get him to spring into action, even if he were the springing-into-action type.

Besides, he probably didn't wear very much when he was sleeping.

She crawled back into bed, switched off the light and closed her eyes. She was immediately assaulted by an image of Keith's cottage blowing up right in front of her. That was followed by a good guess as to how Alec would look running stark naked out of this house.

Both visions were equally disconcerting.

Christine switched the light back on and sat up. Obviously she had too much on her mind to get any sleep tonight.

She climbed out of bed, wishing she had a housecoat. Alec had supplied a small, but decent wardrobe—a couple of pairs of shorts, a pair of jeans, a few T-shirts and even some underwear—all, as he'd promised, very respectable. However, he hadn't bought anything that even remotely resembled sleepwear. Christine had found a few men's shirts hanging at the back of the closet and was using one of those as a nightgown. It was far too big—the sleeves hung past her hands and the shirttails almost touched her knees—but it did keep her decently covered.

She padded down the hall to the bathroom and filled a glass with water. She should be taking a cold shower instead, she thought as she drank it. Maybe that would fix whatever was wrong with her.

She smiled wryly at her reflection, opened the bathroom door and found herself staring directly at a bare male chest. She choked back a startled scream when she realized it was Alec, propped up against the hall wall directly across from her, wearing nothing more than a pair of brown boxer shorts and a frown. "What's wrong?" he asked.

Christine stared at the mat of dark brown hair covering his chest, then followed it down to where it arrowed into the waistband of his boxers. "W-wrong?"

"Yeah." Alec straightened and took a step toward her. "You've been up and down this hall all night. Aren't you feeling well?"

Right now she was a little light-headed, but that was mostly from finding a half-naked man on the other side of the bathroom door. Christine dragged her gaze back up to his face and swallowed. "I'm fine."

His forehead furrowed with confusion. "If you're fine, why aren't you asleep?"

"I, uh..." She eyed the breadth of his shoulders and her mouth went dry again. "I guess I've just got a lot on my mind."

Even when he was half-asleep his eyes sparkled teasingly. "Like what?"

Let's see. Someone was trying to kill her, she felt as if she didn't have a friend in the world and she was alone in the middle of nowhere with a man who thought she belonged in the nuthouse. He didn't think they were in any danger, but she expected a horde of villainous creeps to break into the house any second. Even worse, she was tremendously attracted to this guy and would dearly love to rip off his boxer shorts so she could see what was beneath.

The list was far too long to go into. "It doesn't really matter," Christine hedged. "I'm sorry I woke you. I..." The house creaked, and she shot an uneasy glance toward the staircase before looking back at him. "I just, uh..."

Alec's quizzical expression changed to one of comprehension. "Ah," he said. The green flecks in his eyes sparkled at her. "A little nervous, are we?"

If he started laughing at her right now, she'd probably burst into tears. Christine bit her lip, horrified to realize how close she was to falling apart. "Of course I'm nervous," she snapped. "Someone is trying to kill me. Naturally, I'm a little nervous about it. I have a—a strong aversion to being b-blown up."

His lips rose at one corner. "No one's going to—"

"I don't want to get shot, either." Christine swiped a hand across her face. "I don't want to get run over and I don't want people attacking me."

Alec unfolded his arms and straightened. "No one—"

"I don't want to be in a strange house that makes all kinds of noises with a man I hardly know who thinks I'm crazy." She blinked furiously at his blurry figure. "I want my life back. I know you don't think it's much of a life, but it's mine and I want to be alive to live it."

"You're going to be," Alec promised. He put his arms around her and eased her head to his chest. "Nothing is going to happen to you."

Christine resisted for a moment, then slumped against him. His skin was warm under her cheek, his embrace tremendously comforting. She felt his body stir against her, but he did nothing other than hold her.

After a few minutes she raised her head and moved away from him. "I'm sorry," she said, a little embarrassed by her actions. "I guess I'm more nervous than I thought."

"It's okay. I imagine the damsel in distress is always a little nervous the first night of her rescue." He draped an arm around her shoulders and turned toward her bedroom. "Come on. Let's get you back to bed."

Christine took a few deep breaths and let him guide her. He held back the covers of her bed while she climbed in, tucked them tightly across her shoulders, then sat down beside her. "You are hereby confined to your room for the next eight hours," he announced. "That's the penalty for worrying about our safety when you're not supposed to. It's my responsibility to handle that."

Christine lowered her eyelids. She knew she was the one who had to handle that, because he didn't believe there was anything to worry about. However, there wasn't much point in arguing with him about it.

"There really isn't anything to worry about," Alec continued. "There isn't a soul in the world who knows where you are. Besides, the only way someone can get here is to drive down that gravel road. Since I can't sleep through you wandering up and down the hall, I'm confident that I'm not going to sleep through the sound of a car approaching." He took a breath. "However, if it will make you feel better, I'm perfectly willing to stay up all night and stand guard."

In his boxer shorts? Christine didn't think that would scare away very many bad guys. However, it could attract a lot of women.

She smiled at the thought. "That's not necessary," she assured him. "I'm not nervous anymore."

She wasn't, either—unless that unfamiliar flutter in her tummy was caused by nerves.

6

CHRISTINE THOUGHT Alec would be the type to sleep late and wake up grumpy.

However, she was wrong on at least one count. He was sitting at the kitchen table eating cereal when she came down the next morning. Christine paused in the doorway, surprised by the rush of pleasure she got from seeing him there. It was comforting to know that today there was going to be another person around—especially one who looked as delicious as he did.

Delicious and a little wild. Everything he owned seemed to be wrinkled and worn. This morning he had on an old pair of gray sweat shorts that reached his knees and an equally old, once-white T-shirt with the sleeves ripped out. He'd obviously showered—he had damp hair curling around his neck, and even from across the room she could smell the soap he'd used. He hadn't shaved, and there was an aura of casual disreputability around him that was incredibly attractive.

He looked up and frowned when she entered the room. "I thought I said eight hours."

"What?"

"From two o'clock until eight o'clock is only six hours. I told you that you were confined to your room for eight hours. You should still be sleeping."

"I did sleep," Christine insisted. She'd fallen into a deep sleep almost as soon as he'd left her room. It hadn't been a dreamless sleep, though. His good-looking, humor-filled face had paraded through her dreams most of the night. "Besides, I'm anxious to get to work," she added.

"Work?" Alec rose from his chair and carried his cereal bowl over to the sink. "The distressed damsel doesn't work. She rests and relaxes, and doesn't do much of anything—other than cut the grass, cook and tell her rescuer how wonderful he is."

Christine crossed the kitchen to pour herself a cup of coffee. "*This* damsel works."

"Oh?" Alec rested his back against the counter. "What sort of work do you have in mind?"

Had he forgotten what they were supposed to be doing? "Finding out who's after me."

"Oh, that." He turned to pour more coffee into his own cup. "You aren't going to have anything to do with that. It's my job as official rescuer. Your job is to take it easy."

Christine frowned at his back. "I'm not going to—"

"Yes, you are." He faced her and took a sip of his coffee. "You're my responsibility now. You have to do as I say."

Christine's spine stiffened. "Now, look here, Alec,

if you think you're going to spend this...this rescue bossing me around..."

"Of course that's what I think. During a rescue the *rescuer* is in charge, and the *rescuee* gets bossed around." He shrugged helplessly. "I can't do anything about it. That's just the way these things work."

Christine wasn't sure if she was going to laugh or hurl her coffee at him. "This rescue is going to be different. For one thing, I'm not going to just sit around while you—"

"You don't have to sit around. You can always cut the grass." She tightened her lips and he sighed. "Look, Chrissy, there isn't anything *for* you to do. I'm going to be on the phone most of the day. The only thing you could do is watch, and I won't let you. I don't work with an audience."

Christine wasn't convinced he'd work at all if she didn't keep after him. "I'll take notes."

"I take my own notes."

"Then I'll—"

Alec held up a hand. "It's against the rules for you to argue with me."

Christine gritted her teeth. "I am getting really, really tired of your rules, Alec!"

Alec grinned cheerfully. "Complaining about the rules is also against the rules." He set his cup on the counter, snagged the back of her head with one hand and pulled her to him. His head came down, his cheek scraped against her own and his mouth brushed across hers. Then, before she could even object, he'd released her and was calmly picking up his coffee cup.

Christine gasped in a breath, glowering at him. "I don't think you need to do any more research."

"Oh, that wasn't a research kiss," Alec explained very, very innocently. "It was a penalty kiss."

"What?"

"It's the penalty for complaining about the rules. If the damsel in distress complains about the rules, she has to give the knight in shining armor a kiss. I'm sure I read that somewhere." He grinned smugly, patted her cheek and picked up his cup. "Now, you go relax while I get to work."

"RELAX!" Christine grumbled. "How am I supposed to relax when someone is trying to kill me?"

She stood on the front porch and glared over her shoulder at the house. She knew exactly why Alec wanted her to rest and relax. He was hoping that if she got relaxed enough, she'd forget about the idea that someone was after her. Well, she had bad news for him. That simply wasn't going to happen. For one thing, she knew very well that her life was in danger. And for another, she really stank at resting and relaxing.

She sat down on the porch steps, feeling very much at loose ends. It wasn't that she was incapable of doing it. She seldom had spare time on her hands. Even when she'd been at Keith's cottage she'd had a briefcase full of work with her. She wasn't used to doing nothing.

She also wasn't used to leaving someone else to solve her problems. She gave the house another disgusted glower before propping her chin in her hands. She could always march in there and demand to assist him, but she doubted it would do any good. He'd just think up another stupid rule or ridiculous penalty. Besides, there didn't seem to be much she *could* do to assist. She was just going to have to hope Alec managed to find out something.

She also hoped he discovered it soon. He was an extremely attractive man, he was certainly a good kisser and he'd been very kind to her last night. She didn't want to end up number 312 on the list of women who had slept with him this month.

Apparently she didn't have to worry about that. He'd told her he had no designs on her body—and it seemed that he didn't. All he'd done was kiss her a couple of times. One of those had been a research kiss and the other had been a punishment. Even last night, when they'd been together half-naked in the hallway, all he'd done was hold her. It was almost insulting. He was a known womanizer, and she was the only woman around. Shouldn't he be at least remotely interested?

Christine gave her head an impatient shake. She didn't want him to have any designs on her. She just wanted him to solve this mystery so she could get back to work. She rested her head against the porch railing and tried to think of someone who might have a motive for doing her in. After a few minutes, she gave up. She couldn't think of anyone, and in the bright sunshine it was almost impossible to believe there was someone.

Almost impossible, but not quite. Christine shoved away the disquieting thoughts and stretched to her feet. The grass did need cutting. According to Alec that was something she was allowed to do.

She wandered out to the back shed to see what sort of lawn mower this Marty character owned.

ALEC HUNG UP THE PHONE and watched through the back window as Christine hauled out the lawn mower. The sight made him smile. Apparently she'd taken his "the rescuee has to mow the lawn" idea seriously.

That wasn't surprising. Christine seemed to take everything seriously. After their conversation last night, it was clear she was a class-A workaholic. First she'd devoted herself to her golfing career. Then she'd devoted herself to this health-food thing. She was so busy with her responsibilities, she hardly knew what her own brother did with his spare time! It was no wonder she'd cracked up.

If she'd cracked up.

Alec raised a hand to rub the prickles on the back of his neck. Nothing Christine had told him last night had sounded remotely close to a real murder motive. However, he was still glad he'd chosen this room for his office. That way he could keep an eye on her.

He returned to his seat, shaking his head at the notion. This morning he felt more protective toward her than ever. Maybe some of her nervousness last night had transmitted itself to him. He'd had trouble falling asleep after leaving her room. He'd kept thinking he heard noises.

That wasn't the only reason he couldn't sleep. That hot "research" kiss they'd shared had definitely aroused him. Holding her soft, warm almost-naked body hadn't done anything to alleviate that situation. If she'd been anyone else, he would have done a lot more than try to make her feel safe.

However, Chrissy wasn't anyone else. Last night she'd been extremely vulnerable. Taking advantage of that wouldn't have been right.

Besides, Alec doubted that she'd have let anything happen between them. Christine was not like the other women who had drifted through his bedroom. They were just with him to have a good time, which was the same reason he was with them. Chrissy didn't do things that way. She had to be emotionally involved with someone before she got physically involved. She had to spend a lot of time with him, get to know him.

Of course, after a few days, she would know Alec pretty well. Then...

Then what? She'd get involved with him? He gave his head a disgusted shake. He didn't go around getting *involved* with women! He just...had fun with them. Besides, he was supposed to be rescuing Christine, not seducing her.

On the other hand, maybe that was the sort of rescuing Chrissy needed. After all, a year without sex would make anyone a little uptight.

THAT NIGHT Christine demanded a progress report—assuming Alec had made some progress. "You must have found out something," she insisted as soon as he sat down for dinner. "You were on the phone all day."

"I was," Alec agreed. He took a forkful of the unfamiliar casserole she'd spooned onto his plate and paused before he put it into his mouth. "What is this?"

"A recipe of your aunt's. I found some of her cookbooks when I was cleaning the kitchen. Who did you talk to?"

"A lot of people." He took a tentative taste of the stuff and chewed cautiously. "This isn't bad. What's in it?"

"Potato chips, pretzels, Cheezies and beer," Christine responded promptly. She popped a forkful of it into her own mouth and gave him a wide-eyed, guileless smile. "It has no nutritional value whatsoever and I'm sure it's very bad for you. Now, will you stop worrying that I'm going to sneak something healthy into your stomach and tell me what you found out?"

Alec noted the look of exasperation on her face and gave in. "Okay." He fetched his notebook from the dining room, propped it open with the saltshaker and reviewed his notes. "I tracked down some folks at the university who know your brother. He's a thirty-eight-year-old history professor who people describe as pleasant, polite, hard-working and respectable." He glanced up. "Just the sort of brother I'd expect you to have." Christine made a face at him and he continued. "He's never been married, and his hobbies are skiing, traveling and gourmet cooking. No one knew a lot about his financial situation, but he doesn't sound like much of a killer to me."

Christine breathed a relieved sigh. "I knew Keith had nothing to do with this."

Alec paused before continuing. Keith didn't sound like much of a killer, but those were pretty expensive hobbies. Maybe...

"Go on," Christine said encouragingly.

Alec gave his head a small shake and traced down his notes with a finger. "I sent a number of E-mails to sportswriters who cover the golfing scene, asking if they remember anyone having any sort of a grudge against you. So far, no one can think of anything or anyone, but they'll be getting back to me." He grinned across the table at her. "They do all agree you've got really great knees."

Christine flushed slightly. She looked better today than she had yesterday, Alec noted. The tension on her face had eased a little, and the fearful expression was gone from her eyes. He couldn't recall seeing eyes that particular shade of gray before. After he'd kissed her, they'd been a darker color. After making love, they'd probably be so dark...

"And?"

Alec dragged his mind back from the interesting image he'd been creating. He glanced at her and frowned briefly. He'd had more than one little daydream like this in the last while. It was rather galling to realize that she didn't have the same problem.

He took another look at his notes. "I talked to Johan Wallenburg, the *Centennial* business guru, about this health-food business. He says that HoleSum has increased their market share over the past couple of years. However, he didn't think bumping you off would change that." Alec wasn't so sure. He leaned back in his chair to gauge Chrissy's response.

"It wouldn't," Christine agreed. "If something happened to me, HoleSum would just get someone else."

It was a good point. Alec shoved away his suspicions and continued. "I also spoke with a couple of people at HoleSum Foods about you." He chuckled as he recalled the conversations. "They said exactly the same things about you as people said about Keith. You're hard-working, respectable and polite."

"Go on," Christine encouraged.

Alec shook his head. "That's about it."

"That's it?" Christine's eyebrows rose along with her voice. "It took all day for you to find out that Keith and I are polite?"

Alec snapped his notebook closed, stung by her attitude. He'd already put in more hours on this than he had on any story in recent memory. Even Harper would have been impressed. Apparently, Chrissy wasn't. "Complete villain identification is seldom accomplished in one day, Chrissy."

"I guess not." She caught her bottom lip with her teeth, and her shoulders drooped. "I was just hoping someone would come out of the woodwork, announce that I'm a real bitch and that they couldn't stand me."

Alec doubted that would happen. The HoleSum people hadn't just told him that she was polite. They'd also mentioned that Chrissy worked extraordinarily hard. She took on far more public appearances than her job required, simply because they were for a good cause. In spite of her hectic schedule, she managed to keep up-to-date on everything that was happening in the HoleSum marketing department.

Now he was more positive than ever that stress was her problem, not some mythical assassin. However, she looked so despondent that he found himself reassuring her. "I've got lots of people to talk to yet. I could find dozens of folks who want to do you in."

Christine gave him a wry smile, then rose from the table and picked up their plates. "I really need to get back to work. That carrot-extract campaign has some real problems. And then there's the budget for the next quarter...." She ran water into the sink, then turned to face him. "You must have fax software in that computer. I could get them to—"

"No way!" Alec interrupted. Chrissy was not going to spend her time working! "Rescues do not involve carrots in any shape or form—or budgets, either." He watched her lips form a frown and continued. "Besides, you'd have to tell someone the phone number here, and they could trace you from that. We don't want anyone finding out the location of our hideaway."

Christine looked as if she was about to argue, then changed her mind. "I suppose you're right." She nibbled on a thumbnail. "I could have put in a little practice if my clubs hadn't blown up in that fire. I had them with me for years, you know." She mourned their loss for a moment, then eyed him hopefully. "I don't suppose Marty has—"

"No, he doesn't."

"Is there someplace around here where I could...?"

Alec shook his head. "No."

"There must be," Christine insisted. "I need to

practice. I'm in a charity tournament next week. I don't want to be rusty."

"It doesn't matter if you're rusty. It's just for charity, Chrissy. People come to those things to have fun. All you have to do is show up, look famous and hand out free samples of tofu."

"That's not the point. I—"

"It doesn't matter what the point is. You can't practice here. It's against the rules. No golfing while you're in hiding. Everyone knows that."

Christine's features grew positively mutinous. "Oh, for heaven sakes, Alec! What difference does it make to you if I practice?"

Alec had never seen her look relaxed with a golf club in her hand. However, he didn't think she'd like hearing that. He searched around for another explanation. "I don't think it's safe," he improvised. "The only place to hit a few balls around is on the other side of those trees. I wouldn't be able to see you from in here."

"What does that have to do—"

"It's another rule. The rescuer has to keep an eye on his charge at all times." He carried his glass over to the sink. "Besides, you're supposed to be resting and relaxing, not golfing."

Christine gave him a resentful glare. "It doesn't matter how much I relax. I'm still going to know that someone is trying to kill me." She picked up a dishcloth and wiped viciously at a spot on the counter. "Besides, golf is relaxing."

Alec rested a shoulder against the fridge and watched the movement of her fingers. "The last time I saw you with a golf club in your hand, you didn't look all that relaxed. And it didn't do anything for my nerves, either."

Christine's cheekbones colored. "Those were unusual circumstances."

"I'm still not trusting you anywhere near a golf club." Christine's lips tightened into a straight line and he sighed. "Come on, Chrissy. There must be something you can do around here to relax."

Christine opened her mouth as if to argue, then appeared to change her mind. "Well...I wouldn't mind trying to do something about that yard."

Alec wasn't sure he liked the sound of that. "Like what? Landscaping it?"

"It certainly could use landscaping." She frowned with disapproval. "Honestly, Alec, the way Marty has neglected this place is absolutely disgraceful. There used to be a lovely garden out back. And the flowers..." She shook her head. "If he'd just kept it up, it would be gorgeous. Now it needs a lot of work." She bit down on her lip, obviously taken with the idea. "If you don't think Marty would mind, I'd like to do something about it. My Dad loved to garden. He grew a lot of vegetables and flowers. I used to

like helping him." She sighed. "I haven't done much
of it for years."

It sounded to Alec as if she hadn't done much of
anything except work for a number of years. And if
she thought this was fun… "I'm sure Marty wouldn't
mind. Just don't overdo it. You're supposed to be relaxing, remember?"

"I am getting heartily sick of the word *relax!*"
Christine all but threw the dishcloth into the sink. "I
don't see how I can relax when someone is trying to
do me in!"

Alec studied her tense, angry figure and felt an almost irresistible urge to take her upstairs, spend an
hour removing her clothes and another hour making
love to her until she did tell him he was wonderful.
That would definitely relax *him!*

However, considering her views on casual sex
and her decidedly temperamental disposition, he
doubted she'd welcome the suggestion. "Well," he
said thoughtfully, "I suppose we could always try
football."

"I DON'T WANT TO WATCH a football game," Christine
objected as Alec guided her into the living room. "I
don't find watching television relaxing, I don't need
to relax anyway and…and you should be working."

Alec propelled her over to the sofa and sat down.
"You might work twenty-six hours a day, but I don't.
Besides, all rescues involve football in one form or an-

other. You might as well face it now and get it over with."

"Oh," Christine said. "Well, uh..." She watched him swing his bare feet up onto the footstool and gave up. Clearly, he'd done as much work as he was going to do for one day. Plus there was little point in arguing with him when he was in the mood to make rules. "All right," she conceded. "But I don't really know very much about football."

Alec arched an eyebrow in her direction. "You don't know much about football?" He shook his head, his eyes sparkling with laughter. "I suppose if sex isn't a priority for you, football isn't, either."

Christine gave him a resentful glare and started to rise. "If you're going to start that again..."

"Easy, Chrissy, easy." Alec caught her arm and tugged her back down. "Just sit down, relax, and I'll explain it to you." He patted her arm bracingly. "You don't even have to pay close attention because there isn't going to be a test." He picked up a huge remote-control device, adroitly punched in a zillion codes, and soon a satellite picture appeared on the television screen.

Much to her own surprise, Christine did relax. It was impossible to remain annoyed with Alec for very long—especially with his thigh pressed against hers and his arm resting lightly across her shoulders. He explained the game in a lighthearted, amusing, easy-to-understand fashion, teased her about her lack of knowledge, and by the time the game ended, Christine realized she had enjoyed herself.

"That was interesting," she announced as he used the remote to mute the television. She studied him with new respect. "You really do know a lot about football."

Alec took a handful of potato chips from the bowl on his lap and popped one in his mouth. "I've been a sports reporter for almost a decade. I should know something about sports."

Christine shifted her body so she was facing him, one of her legs curled under her. "Is that what you always wanted to do?"

"Pretty much." Alec took a healthy swig from the beer can in his hand before continuing. "I always enjoyed sports—and I could bullshit my way through an English class without too many problems. Sports reporting seemed like a natural choice."

Christine eyed his decidedly athletic-looking body. "You never considered playing professionally yourself?"

"Me?" Alec gave his head a quick side-to-side shake. "Good God, no! Oh, I suppose when I was a kid I might have wanted to become a world-famous athlete, but I soon got over it when I discovered how hard they had to work."

Christine sensed an implied criticism and tensed. "Everyone has to work hard at something, Alec. The reporters that followed the tour didn't have it much easier than we did. They had to travel as much, watch everything...and when we were finished playing, they had to rush around interviewing people, making their deadline...."

"Yeah, but we don't have to practice and we don't have curfews. And once the story is done, we're free to do whatever we like."

That was true, Christine conceded. The press group always seemed to have time to party and socialize, while the athletes had to concentrate on their game.

"Professional athletes have to work too hard," Alec continued. "They take their sport so seriously that they get all stressed out. Then they don't enjoy what they're doing anymore."

Christine narrowed her eyes. "If you're referring to me, that's simply not true. I admit it was hard work, but I didn't mind it. I really liked the tour."

Privately, though, she wasn't so sure that was true. The first years she'd played she had enjoyed it. However, the last few she certainly hadn't. It had seemed like the more she won, the more pressure she'd put on herself to win. Maybe she had been more stressed out about it than she thought.

"What about now?" Alec asked. "Can you really say you enjoy that horrible schedule of yours?"

"There are some parts of it I enjoy, yes." Not a whole lot, when she thought about it. She did enjoy her work setting up the children's sports programs. But the rest of it—the extensive travel, the public appearances, the "hocking bean sprouts"—well, she didn't get much enjoyment out of that. However, it was those things that made the other things possible. "Besides, there's more to life than enjoying yourself."

"Like what? Fame and money?" Alec shook his head. "I'm not into that, thanks."

"I was thinking along the lines of challenges and accomplishments. Or aren't you into those, either?"

Alec's jaw tightened a minuscule amount. "I've accomplished something. I've got my own column."

"And you're content with that."

"Yes, I am. I like my life just fine the way it is. I enjoy watching sports, and someone pays me to do it. All I have to do in return is write a few lines about it. I like what I do, I don't have to work too hard, I don't take it too seriously, I don't get all stressed out about it and I have plenty of time to enjoy myself."

Enjoying himself seemed to be Alec's major preoccupation. And there was something appealing about his laid-back life-style. It was a direct contrast to her own busy schedule. Maybe she did work a little too hard sometimes—and maybe she was too dedicated to it.

But he wasn't dedicated enough! "If all you care about is enjoying yourself, what on earth possessed you to help me?"

Alec shrugged a shoulder. "I felt I should."

Christine watched him take another sip of beer. "Why?"

"I just did." His lips turned down at the corners as he concentrated on the beer can, turning it around and around in his palms. "It's partly my fault you're in this situation. I want to make up for that—even if it's only to give you peace of mind." He turned his head toward her. "Besides, I don't want anything to happen to you."

His gaze met hers. For a moment he looked very serious indeed. Then he winked, grinned and raised the beer can again to drain it. "After all, I wouldn't want anything to happen to someone with knees like yours."

"YOUR HEALTHY WAYS must be getting to me," Alec complained as he walked her up the stairs later. "I usually go through a lot more than one tiny bowl of potato chips and one can of beer." He stopped in front of her bedroom door and grinned teasingly down into her face. "Of course, I saw you sneak a few handfuls of potato chips."

"I only had a couple," Christine retorted defensively. "And don't you dare tell anyone. The HoleSum Foods lady does not eat potato chips."

"You don't have to worry about that," Alec assured her. "This entire arrangement is off the record—unless I identify a heinous villain, of course. Then I want an exclusive." He rested an outstretched arm against the wall and studied her face. "You're not going to be nervous tonight, are you?"

Christine shook her head.

"If you do get nervous or if you think you hear something, call me." He stroked a finger along her cheek. "Or if you'd rather, you're welcome to spend the night in my bed. I guarantee you won't be nervous there."

The twinkle in his eye indicated he was teasing, although the idea increased Christine's heart rate to an almost painful degree. "That's, uh, okay," she said. "I'm not at all nervous."

"If you change your mind, you know where I'll be." He bent forward and softly brushed his lips across hers before turning in the direction of his room.

Christine sucked in a breath and watched as he strolled down the hall. "Alec?"

He turned around.

"You do remember that this is going to be a...a platonic rescue."

"A platonic rescue?" He rested a shoulder against the wall while he considered her. "What makes you think this is going to be a platonic rescue?"

"You did," Christine reminded him. "At the hospital. You said you didn't have any designs on my body."

"Oh, that!" Alec shrugged eloquently. "I lied about that. It's one of those rescue things. The rescuer always has designs on the rescuee's body, and he always lies about it. I thought you knew that. All rescues involve heavy breathing and hot sex. Why else would knights face fifty-foot-tall, fire-breathing dragons to rescue damsels in distress?"

He grinned and straightened. "Don't look so alarmed, Chrissy. I was just trying to give you something to think about tonight other than our safety."

7

"THEY *WERE SO* BEANS," Alec accused a couple of evenings later.

He held open the screen door for Christine to pass through, then let it bang behind them. "You might give them some sort of weird-sounding French name, but I'm positive they were beans."

Christine sank into one of the green lawn chairs on the porch and tried not to giggle at his disgruntled expression. Over the past couple of days Alec had grown increasingly suspicious of the meals she'd served him. She'd had to get more and more creative to sneak something healthy into his stomach. "You ate them."

"That's because you bribed me with chocolate cake!" He sat sprawled on a chair across from her, his legs stretched out in front of him. He shaved sporadically, but always seemed to have a partial growth of beard around his chin. His choice of clothes didn't vary much beyond sweat shorts and a loose T-shirt. Today he had on a pair of blue shorts and a black T-shirt with a tear in the hem. He looked devilish, disreputable...and very, very sexy. "Where did you get those beans, anyway?" he asked. "I didn't buy any."

"I found them in the garden." Christine watched his fingers curl around the handle of his coffee cup, and her body warmed from within. She was having a tremendous problem getting Alec's heavy-breathing-and-hot-sex statement out of her mind. He made it worse. Every time he made a teasing sexual innuendo, brushed his lips lightly across hers in one of his kissing penalties or draped a casual arm around her shoulders, she thought about it again.

And she was coming to the conclusion that it might not be such a bad thing to have happen. True, Alec wasn't the type for a long-term relationship, but she'd already concluded that she wasn't interested in one. She wouldn't mind a short-term relationship, though. Alec wasn't the creep she'd initially thought he was. He was a decent guy—a little too laid-back, perhaps, but still a person with a conscience. He felt badly about what he'd done, and he was trying to make up for it. He did appear to be working hard on solving this problem for her, and he seemed genuinely concerned about her well-being. That could be because he thought she was a basket case, but every now and then she got the distinct impression there was more to it than that.

She took a long breath of the cool night air and leaned forward to set her coffee cup on the table, wincing at a twinge in her right shoulder.

"What's the matter?" Alec demanded.

"I'm just a little stiff." She massaged her shoulder. "I guess gardening uses different muscles than golf."

His lips formed into a frown. "You're not supposed to be using your muscles, Chrissy! You are supposed to be relaxing!"

Christine made a face at the word. She'd heard it a lot over the past couple of days. Alec was absolutely determined to get her to relax. He kept a close eye on what she was doing, and if it looked too strenuous, he made up a rule about it. He absolutely refused to work after dinner. Instead they watched sporting events on television or sat on the porch and talked. Although Christine could sometimes shake him for his nonchalant attitude, she had to admit she was enjoying all this attention. It had been years since someone had taken care of her.

And she was relaxing, probably more than she should. Their conversation the other night had made her realize that she'd never get him to take her seriously if she acted like a stressed-out workaholic. She was doing everything she could think of to prove him wrong. She worked in the garden. She went through his aunt's cookbooks, trying out new recipes and doing her best to fool Alec into eating properly. She read thrillers. It was completely different from her usual schedule, and…it was fun.

It was a rescue mission, she reminded herself. It wasn't supposed to be fun. Remembering that, though, was getting harder and harder. She straightened. "And how did your day go?"

"Ah, yes. The nightly news report." Alec smiled briefly, then focused on his notebook. "I spent all day talking to people about this health-food stuff. It's big business, Chrissy."

"Yes, I know. I—"

"SportsNuts Health Food seems to be the big loser. Their profits are down considerably."

"That's more because of the product than anything else," Christine explained. "Their low-sodium frozen vegetables are distinctly mushy. And then there's the packaging." She made a face. "Whoever thought of blue-and-black labels made a big mistake. People don't want to eat something from a can that looks like a bruise."

Alec chuckled at that. "That was most likely the brainchild of the vice president of marketing, Robert Shultzer. Apparently he's the guy getting all the blame for SportsNuts's poor showing." He glanced up. "Do you know him?"

Christine had a vague recollection of a black-haired, narrow-faced man. "I run into him from time to time at trade shows. He seems pleasant enough. As a matter of fact, the last time I saw him he..." She stopped talking as she suddenly remembered who she'd been with when she'd seen him.

"What?" Alec asked. "When was the last time you saw him?"

"In June. In San Diego," Christine admitted. "He was on the beach and..."

"You were on a beach?" Alec's eyes sparkled teasingly. "What were you doing? Reading marketing reports?"

"Not exactly," Christine muttered, although it was a fairly accurate description.

The blue in his eyes gleamed with curiosity. "Were you alone?"

No, she'd been with Estelle, but she didn't want Alec to know that. "Yes." Christine blinked a couple of times. "Surely you don't think Mr. Shultzer would..."

"I doubt it," Alec admitted. "He told me that although you worked for the competition, he felt that your serious, respectable image had improved the public perception of health food and generated more revenue for the industry as a whole." He grinned up at her. "Apparently the wheat-germ business is going great."

Christine's spirits plummeted. "Terrific," she muttered. She heaved an enormous sigh. "You know, Alec, this is getting really depressing."

Alec snapped his notebook shut, rested his head back against the chair and groaned. "The word *wonderful* just isn't in your vocabulary, is it?" he mumbled.

"What?"

"Never mind." He sighed. "What's depressing you

today? You think I should have talked to another three hundred people in the past eight hours?"

"Oh, it's not that," Christine assured him. "It's everything. Everyone you've talked to says the same sort of things about me. I'm reliable. Dependable. Polite. Well-organized. Prompt. Even the competition says I'm serious and respectable!"

"You're depressed because people say you're serious and respectable?" One corner of his lip curled. "You should hear what they say about me. Then you'd really be depressed."

"I'm sure it's more exciting than this!" She gave his notebook a disgusted glower. "I sound like one of the most boring people on the planet!"

"Boring?" Alec straightened at that. "You're a lot of things, Chrissy, but boring isn't one of them. You're one of the few Canadians to get a golf scholarship to an American university. You had a distinguished professional golfing career, the sales at HoleSum have increased fifteen percent since you've been there and then there are the children's programs you've organized. You've accomplished an awful lot for someone who doesn't eat junk food."

Christine's pulse rate increased, both at his words and at the honest admiration in his face. "Thank you," she said. "That's a nice thing to say. But none of that should motivate someone to want to kill me."

"You never know." Alec furrowed his forehead thoughtfully and stared into the distance over her head. "People who accomplish things usually have enemies."

Christine's gaze flew to his face. "Have you found..."

He focused back on her and grinned. "I haven't found out anything—except that you work too hard. Which reminds me." He took a look at his watch. "It's time for you to hit the showers."

"What?"

"You heard me. You have to take a shower now. That stiff shoulder of yours needs some warm water. And then you have to get some sleep. You're worn-out."

"I am not worn-out! And it's not even that late. I—"

"You are worn-out, Chrissy. You got up at the crack of dawn, and you've been digging up the yard ever since. I'm exhausted from watching you, so you must be tired, too. Besides, another rule is that if the rescuee insists on getting up at seven a.m., she has to go to bed early."

"That's ridiculous. I..."

Alec narrowed his eyes, put his hands on the arms of his chair and started to rise. "The penalty for not doing it is that I carry you upstairs and—"

Christine raised her hands in surrender. "All right. I'm going—but only if you promise not to make up any more new rules!"

Alec chuckled and settled back in his chair. "I'm

not promising that. The rescuer has to make up rules. It's one of the rules."

Christine made a face at him and started out of the room. She'd reached the door when Alec spoke her name. "Chrissy?"

She turned around.

"I wouldn't mind livening up your life a little." His voice lowered to a caressing drawl. "And I've got some real interesting ideas on how to do it."

His eyes were as smoky and sultry as his tone. Christine's mouth went dry as she gazed into them. She swallowed a couple of times and struggled for a smile. "Someone is trying to kill me, Alec. I think that's as much livening up as my life needs."

As she wandered up the stairs, though, Christine wondered if either of those statements were really true.

"I'VE BEEN FRANTICALLY worried about you," Estelle admonished. "Where are you? What's going on? The newspaper said—"

"I'm fine," Christine assured her. She took an anxious look up the staircase before speaking into the phone again. She'd risen at six o'clock so she could call Estelle without Alec hearing her do it.

Christine felt guilty about sneaking around, but she'd decided it was necessary. She'd been right in thinking Estelle would be frantically worried about her. Christine should have contacted her days ago.

"I'm, uh, staying with a friend," she continued. She hated lying, but she doubted Estelle would approve of this situation. Besides, it wasn't that much of a lie. Alec was becoming a very good friend.

"What friend?" Estelle asked sharply. "What—"

"It doesn't matter. I'm quite well and—"

"I'd feel so much better if I could see you. Why don't you hop on a plane and fly down here? I'll take very good care of you. And if you're still concerned that your life is in danger, well, we can get someone to investigate that."

"That's kind of you, but—"

"Then I'll come there," Estelle decided. "Where—"

"That's not necessary," Christine interjected. The last thing this setup needed was a psychiatrist showing up in the middle of it. "I'm having a wonderful vacation." That was true, too. She was enjoying herself. "I'm doing exactly what you told me to do. Rest and relax."

Estelle's voice held a hint of skepticism. "Oh? And how are you doing that?"

Gardening, cooking and thinking about sex. Christine didn't think Estelle needed to hear that, either. "The usual things. Budget reports. The carrot-extract campaign. Golf..."

Estelle's tone rose in alarm. "You're not golfing, are you?"

"I..."

"You should not be doing that. It's one of the stress

inducers for compulsive chronic memory syndrome. According to—"

Christine heard a movement from upstairs and panicked. "I have to go, Estelle. I just wanted to tell you not to worry about me."

"Just a minute, Christine. You haven't told me where you are or who you're staying with."

"I'm staying near, uh..." What was the name of that town? "Cremona."

"I'M GOING OUTSIDE to work in the garden," Christine advised Alec the next morning. "I will be where you can see me. I'll be very relaxed while I'm doing it." She tipped the coffeepot to refill his cup. "And if you make up some rule about why I can't do it, I'll serve you fried lima beans for supper tonight."

Alec chuckled and watched the movement of her wrist. Lord, the woman had nice fingers. And those hands, well, they were just as attractive as her knees.

He grasped her wrist, took the coffeepot away from her and pulled her down onto his lap. "That sounds suspiciously like a threat," he growled into her ear. "You know what the penalty is for that?"

Her gaze met his, her eyes wide and luminous. "W-what?"

"Guess." He pressed her face between his palms, holding it still while he touched his lips to hers. She practically melted against him, her mouth opening under his, while she arched her body closer. Her hands closed around his shoulders; she made a soft sound of appreciation....

Then she stiffened and eased herself out of the embrace. Her cheeks were flushed, her lips glistening from his kiss. Her tongue stroked across her bottom lip, and she blinked rapidly. "I, uh, think that's enough of a penalty for one little threat," she said breathlessly. "And I really should get working on that garden."

Alec stifled a groan as he watched her hurry out of the room. He was starting to regret telling her she could work in the yard. She spent more time out there than she did with him!

He wandered into the dining room and frowned moodily at his computer. Christine's comments about his life the other night had been dangerously close to accurate. There weren't a whole lot of challenges in it. When he'd first started in his profession, he had been highly driven. He even used to look forward to working. But for the past few years, he hadn't given his job much more than a passing thought. As a matter of fact, rescuing Christine was the biggest task he'd taken on in a decade—even more of a challenge than he'd expected.

For one thing, it was unusual for him to spend this much time with a woman he wasn't sleeping with, but wanted to be. And there was no question he wanted her. Every second he spent in her company made his desire stronger.

It might be easier if he tried to avoid being around her so much. However, he couldn't seem to help himself. He liked her companionship. He looked forward to mealtimes, not because he particularly enjoyed the food—she still insisted on foisting nutritionally correct meals on him at every opportunity—but because he liked talking to her. He liked hearing about her life, liked arguing about the rules he invented.... The only thing he didn't like was that she went to her own bedroom every night.

So far he hadn't done much to change that, although he was beginning to think he should. He was positive she was as attracted to him as he was to her. She responded when he kissed her, but then she backed away. Her cool manner warded him off. If she'd just get over this involvement hang-up, he was sure they'd both be much better off.

Christine was relaxing, at least to some extent anyway. She looked a lot better, she slept at night and she hadn't mentioned their safety in days. However, no matter how relaxed he got her, she simply refused to believe someone wasn't after her. She just thought Alec hadn't been able to identify the person yet.

This, and the way she insisted on reviewing his notes, suggested that she didn't think Alec was capable of doing a good job. Actually, he figured he was doing a great job. He'd become engrossed in the work. It had been years since he'd put out the effort to dig for a story, and he'd forgotten how much he enjoyed it. He often found himself forgetting that he was looking for someone who didn't exist.

And sometimes he found himself wondering if Christine was right, even though there was no real reason for him to change his mind. Her brother seemed innocuous enough, but he did have an awfully strong motive. Her former competitors claimed to have nothing against her, but they could easily resent the fame she'd received as a result of her job with HoleSum Foods. And there was no question that HoleSum's competition had been hurt financially by her activities.

Apart from that, there was Chrissy herself. Granted, she worked hard, but she insisted that she enjoyed it and couldn't wait to get back to it. As a matter of fact, that seemed to be all she cared about. Besides, she'd been under the same amount of stress for a number of years. Why would she suddenly fall apart now?

Some rescue this was turning out to be. She was relaxing and he was getting paranoid.

ACCORDING TO Estelle Lamont, he wasn't the only one who was paranoid.

"It's what I call chronic compulsive memory syndrome," Estelle explained. "I believe it's very common in former athletes. Now my research has shown they have the potential..."

Alec listened to Estelle's explanation with half his

brain, while the other half was reeling with astonishment.

It had taken him some time to discover that when Christine had visited San Diego, her companion had been a Dr. Estelle Lamont, from Miami. Alec had assumed the person was a man, and had become extremely curious as to why Chrissy hadn't wanted to tell him about her friend.

Now he knew.

"I suspect that's what Christine's problem is," Estelle concluded. She paused. "Of course, I can't make a definite diagnosis without seeing the patient."

"Oh?" Alec said. "So you haven't seen Christine on a professional basis?"

"No, I haven't. I did speak with her after that fire. I tried to convince her to come to my clinic, but...well, Christine just refuses to admit that she has a problem. She kept insisting that her life was in danger. I haven't heard from her since." She paused. "You wouldn't happen to know where she is right now, would you?"

"I haven't seen her recently, no." It wasn't exactly a lie. It had been at least four minutes since she'd been in here. "As I said, I'm just doing a story about her. A little investigative reporting into these things that have happened to her."

"Now is a very bad time to do any sort of a story about Christine," Estelle admonished. "It could be dangerous for her mental health." She lowered her voice confidentially. "Off the record, Mr. O'Brian, Christine is in a very delicate state right now. She never completely recovered from the rigors of life on tour. She works far too hard—and these accidents she's had certainly haven't helped."

Alec scowled at the phone. Estelle made it sound as if Christine was a lot worse off than he thought she was. "You're positive those were just accidents?"

"Of course they were. I realize that isn't the way Christine is interpreting them, but she's simply suffering from a mild case of paranoia. It's one of the symptoms of compulsive chronic memory syndrome. It can be triggered by anything that reminds the patient of former stress. In Christine's case it is most likely related to golf. Green grass. A golf club. Even a crowd."

Alec glanced out the window. Christine was strolling across the lawn. She didn't seem to be freaking out about it. "I've never heard of this chronic memory condition."

"Naturally, you haven't. It hasn't formally been recognized as a syndrome yet. However, I'm confident that will happen very shortly. And I'm almost positive that's Christine's problem. What she needs is rest, relaxation therapy and a gradual reintroduction of the stress factors, in a nonstressful manner. If I could get her to my clinic, I'm positive she would be well on the road to recovery in a matter of weeks. If you do find her, Mr. O'Brian, I'd appreciate it if you'd give me a call immediately. She is in desperate need of my help."

"Right," Alec muttered. "I'll, uh, keep that in mind."

He hung up the phone and thoughtfully tapped his fingers on the tabletop. For some reason that conversation had made him uncomfortable. Estelle had made Christine sound completely around the bend and was so insistent that he not bother investigating her story. Maybe...

He gave his head a slight shake. Chrissy's uneasiness had obviously gotten to him. This psychologist wasn't the villain in her little drama. It appeared no one was.

Now what was he going to do? Should he end this rescue and try to convince Chrissy to go see Dr. Lamont? He didn't see much point in that. Chrissy probably didn't want to go to that clinic or she would have gone already.

He wandered over to the window and leaned against the glass. Chrissy was digging in the garden, no doubt discovering some other weird vegetable in there that she was going to coax him into eating tonight. She was wearing one of his T-shirts, she had dirt on her nose and she didn't look in the least bit unbalanced.

Why should she go to the Lamont clinic for relaxation therapy? She was relaxing quite nicely here, with him. He certainly didn't feel like ending their arrangement right now. He enjoyed being here with her. He liked getting up in the morning with some purpose in mind, knowing that she needed him to take care of her, to solve this for her, to make sure she was all right.

She still needed him. She'd obviously recovered from any negative reaction to "green grass." All he had to do was gradually reintroduce her to the stress factors in a nonstressful manner, and spend a little more effort getting her to take it easy.

There was no reason for his rescue to be over.

8

"I THOUGHT YOU SAID I wasn't allowed to golf," Christine objected.

She swallowed nervously as Alec swung the car into the parking lot of the Cremona golf course. When he'd first suggested this, she'd thought it might be a good idea. She did need the practice. Besides, she needed to prove to herself that she wouldn't fall apart on a golf course.

Now she wished she'd put more thought into it. The last time she'd been on a course, someone had taken a shot at her. What if that someone was here now?

"Golf is allowed if it is done for relaxation only," Alec advised.

Christine rolled her eyes at the word. She'd suspected this was another of Alec's ongoing attempts to get her to unwind. Hopefully, a sane performance here would convince him once and for all that she was not on the verge of a nervous breakdown.

Now she wasn't sure she could give a sane performance. "I don't need more relaxation. And you certainly don't need to go golfing. You should be working."

Alec parked the car and switched off the engine. "I don't work after six."

Christine didn't move. "Someone might see me here."

"There isn't anyone around to see you. There are only three cars in the parking lot. Besides, even if someone saw you, they wouldn't recognize you. You don't look much like the HoleSum Foods lady dressed like that."

Christine glanced down at her attire. She had on her own shorts, but she'd borrowed one of Alec's shirts. Her hair was loose around her shoulders, instead of tied back as she usually wore it, and she probably looked as disreputable as he did. He was right. No one would recognize her.

Alec climbed out and came around to open her door for her. "Come on, Chrissy. It'll be fun."

"Right," Christine muttered. She took an apprehensive look around and got out. There was no reason to be concerned, she told herself. It seemed like a safe-enough thing to do, and no one could know that they'd come here.

Still, she was reluctant to do this. As they strolled toward the clubhouse, she tried one last desperate attempt to get out of it. "I don't play well without my own clubs."

Alec chuckled. "It doesn't matter how well you

play." He dropped a casual arm over her shoulders. "I'm going to win."

Christine couldn't believe his arrogance. "I might be a little rusty, but I did play this professionally. I doubt you could—"

"I'd better," Alec warned. "It's against the rules for the rescuee to beat the rescuer at anything." He stopped walking, pulled her into his arms and bumped his hips suggestively against hers. "And you wouldn't believe the penalty for doing it."

CHRISTINE HAD a pretty good idea what the penalty for doing it was, but as they approached the last hole, she decided she wouldn't mind paying it. As a matter of fact, she was looking forward to it.

She slid her arm around Alec's waist and gave him a grateful hug. "You are not winning, you know," she admonished. "You've been cheating all along. There's a big difference."

He glanced down at her, grinning. "Of course I've been cheating. How else do you expect me to win?"

Christine shook her head at him, but she was smiling. She'd been so apprehensive about playing. Now she was glad she had. She hadn't enjoyed the game this much in a long, long time.

That was all due to Alec, of course. She should have known that playing with him wouldn't be like playing with anyone else. Alec was fun! It was impossible to take any part of the game seriously when he was

teasing her, assigning kissing penalties at every hole
or ambling down the fairway with his arm around
her shoulders. It was too bad she didn't have him
around when she had to do those charity affairs. Then
maybe she'd actually enjoy them.

She took a sideways peek at his profile, a little ap-
palled at how dangerously attached she was getting
to him. Of course he wouldn't be around. This rescue
was going to end in a few days. With any luck, by
then he would have solved this. Maybe now that
she'd proven she wouldn't fall apart on a golf course,
he would stop pestering her to take it easy.

She glanced around before selecting a club. He had
been right about this place. There wasn't much to see
except the green grass and the trees. There wasn't
even another player in sight.

She watched Alec amble toward the rough, where
his ball had landed. As she silently admired the easy,
casual grace of his motions she suddenly realized
something wasn't right.

Her left thumb had twitched.

IF HE EVER GAVE up sportswriting, Alec decided, he
just might take up psychology. He was pretty darn
good at it.

He shoved his hands in his pockets and watched
Christine make the difficult decision about which
club to use. She was a little too intense about this
game. However, she had overcome her initial appre-

hension. She'd relaxed, she'd played well and neither the green grass nor the sight of a golf club had turned her into a screaming basket case. Either he was really great at this shrink stuff or the doctor's diagnosis was completely out to lunch.

Would that mean Chrissy's fears were justified?

The idea gave him a cold chill. Alec stared at a nearby elm while he considered it. The truth was, this game hadn't proved very much. As a matter of fact, it hadn't proved a thing. Sure, she'd been a little nervous when they'd arrived, but at no time had she exhibited any of the "paranoia" Dr. Lamont had described. It could be that he'd gotten Chrissy so relaxed she'd overcome it. But it could also be that she didn't have anything to overcome.

He suddenly realized that Christine was taking an inordinately long amount of time to select a club. He focused on her again. She was standing with her back to him, her shoulders tense, her attitude that of alertness. "Chrissy?"

She turned around. Her face was white, and her eyes were enormous gray pools in her face. "We have to leave, Alec. *Now!*"

"THAT'S THE FIRST TIME I've ever sneaked off a golf course," Alec observed. He shot Christine a puzzled, concerned look before returning his attention to the road. "I'm sort of curious about why I did it."

"I didn't feel safe there," Christine muttered. She

glanced across the front seat at him, then checked the road behind. She didn't blame Alec for wanting to know what was going on, but she couldn't tell him. She wasn't really sure, either. The only thing she did know was that staying on that golf course would have been a direct threat to her health—and possibly Alec's, as well.

She didn't know what form that threat would have taken, or where it had been coming from. She hadn't seen anyone else around. Her thumb had twitched that one time only, and the feeling of unease had almost immediately faded. However, Christine hadn't wanted to take any chances. All she'd wanted to do was get them to safety as quickly as possible. Alec had been pretty understanding about it. He'd put up a couple of objections, then followed her through the trees.

She breathed a sigh of relief as he parked the car in its usual spot behind the house. At least they were safe here. No one had followed them, and...

She paused in midthought. There was always the possibility that someone had been here while they were gone. That's what had happened at Keith's cottage.

Alec switched off the engine and started to open his door. Christine's apprehension returned. He didn't have twitching thumbs to warn him of danger. She did. She put a hand on his arm. "Just a minute, Alec. I, uh, have to go in first."

His forehead wrinkled. "What?"

"I just have to go in first," Christine insisted. She snatched the keys out of his hand, hopped out of the car and darted across the lawn. Nothing happened when she fitted the key into the lock. Nothing happened when she put her hand on the doorknob and took a tentative step inside. And nothing happened when she stood in the kitchen. The place looked exactly as they'd left it. Her feelings of unease didn't return, and nothing twitched.

"Chrissy?"

Christine turned around. Alec was slouched against the kitchen doorway, staring at her as if she had Crazy tattooed across her forehead.

"What was that all about?" he asked.

Christine looked down at her hands. Perhaps she should tell him. His life could be in jeopardy as well. On the other hand, there was very little chance that he'd believe her. Besides, nothing had happened, and she was almost positive they were safe here. "I was just, uh, checking the place," she murmured.

"Checking the place?" He squinted at her. "We were at the golf course and you got an irresistible urge to check the house?"

Christine flushed and averted her eyes. "No, of course not. I just didn't feel safe on that golf course, Alec. I think there could have been some-thing…dangerous there."

"There wasn't anything dangerous there," Alec insisted. "There was no one else around. Besides, no one knows where you are."

Christine sat in the exact middle of the couch and watched him pace back and forth across the living room. She was unaccountably annoyed with him. She realized how irrational her statement sounded. On the other hand, it wasn't totally improbable. "Someone could have figured it out."

"How?"

Good question. Christine chewed on her bottom lip. "I don't know." She blinked away tears of reaction, relief and frustration. "I never should have gone to a public course in the first place. I don't know what on earth possessed me to do it. Something could have happened...."

Alec sat down beside her and put his arm around her. "Nothing happened, Chrissy." His lips flickered in a teasing smile. "And you're not supposed to be worrying about our safety. I'm the rescuer around here. I get to do neat stuff like that."

"But you're not doing it! If you were, you wouldn't have dragged me to that golf course in the first place! Someone is trying to kill me, Alec! It's no time to walk out into the middle of a golf course."

Alec stroked his hand soothingly up and down her arm. "No one is trying to kill you."

Christine stiffened at that. She glanced up at him. "I thought you were keeping an open mind."

"I have kept an open mind. I just haven't found anything to back up your claim."

Christine's stomach sank with dismay. He wasn't going to give up because of this, was he? "Then you must have missed something!"

He eased her head back against him. "I haven't missed anything. No one is trying to kill you. If you'd just loosen up you'd realize that."

"But I have loosened up, Alec! You've made me relax and relax and relax, and I still know that someone is trying to kill me."

Alec stroked a finger down her cheek. "Maybe you just haven't loosened up in the right way."

His tone was soft and low, and the touch of his finger on her face incredibly arousing. "What do you mean?"

"There is one thing we haven't tried." He used a finger under her chin to raise her head. "Maybe it's time we did." His lips brushed hers in a kiss as gentle as the summer breeze wafting through the window.

Christine made no effort to resist. His embrace was comforting, the feel of his lips familiar. It was just one of his light, teasing kisses...and they'd done that often enough. This time, though, the suction of his mouth increased. His hand curled around the back of her neck, then caressed down, feathering across a breast, pulling her closer and closer to him.

Then he was easing her down so her head rested on the arm of the sofa. His mouth trailed a line of kisses down her throat, while he covered a breast with one of his hands, drew circles around the peak with a finger, then squeezed the nipple through the material of her shirt. Christine gasped at the rush of pleasure created by his touch. "That's right, Chrissy," he murmured encouragingly. "Just let go."

Maybe that's what she should do. Maybe she should simply let it all go, just let this happen.

He pushed aside the material of her shirt and pressed his lips to the curve of her breast. Christine arched instinctively, then stiffened and gazed down at the top of his head. "Just a minute, Alec. Is that why you're doing this? To get me to unwind?"

Alec raised his face enough so that his gaze met hers, the blue in his eyes dark and sensuous. "What difference does it make why we do it? We're both enjoying it." He lowered his head to nuzzle her again. "And it just might help."

Christine felt as if she'd been doused with a bucket of cold water. "What are you suggesting—a little sex therapy for the crazy lady?" She gave him an enormous shove, pushing him onto the floor, and scrambled to her feet. "Well, you can forget that!"

Alec blinked up at her. "What...?"

Christine gathered the edges of her shirt together into a fist, her hand trembling with her anger. "I am *not* going to sleep with you in order to relax!"

"I—"

"For one thing, I don't need to relax! As a matter of

fact, I shouldn't! I am far too relaxed already. I am so relaxed I let you take me to the middle of a golf course, where I could have been killed!" Her voice rose. "Maybe that's what it's going to take to convince you that my life is in danger."

Alec pushed himself to his feet. "Your life isn't—"

"Not that you'd care. All you want to do is prove that I'm some sort of nervous wreck because I work too hard. Then you'd have a convenient excuse for not finding the killer."

Alec's mouth turned down derisively at the corners. "That's not true. I have worked hard on this. I haven't found anything!"

"That's because you've been so busy trying to get me to forget my worries that you haven't put any effort into it!" She waved her hands in the air, more furious than she'd ever been in her life. "You were even willing to make love to me to prove your point." She ground her teeth together. "How exactly was that supposed to work? Was I supposed to wake up tomorrow morning and say, 'Wow! Now that I've slept with Alec O'Brian, I realize I must have been crazy!'" She glowered at him. "Well, come to think of it, I would have been crazy to sleep with the likes of you."

Alec held up both hands in surrender. "Hey, I wasn't doing anything you didn't want me to do." He took a step toward her. "You seemed to be enjoying yourself."

Christine backed away from him. "That's not the point! I don't go to bed with men in order to relax! I have to be emotionally involved before I get physically involved, and I have no intention of getting involved with you, period! So how about if you stop fooling around, stop trying to get me to loosen up and do what you said you'd do—find out who is after me?" She put her hands on her hips. "Or have you decided that one of the rules of this rescue is that I have to sleep with you?"

Alec's eyes narrowed and his jaw tightened. Then he blinked a couple of times and laughed. He actually put back his head and laughed—a soft, mocking sound that grated on her nerves like fingernails on a blackboard. "Ah, Chrissy. You're the only person I know who gets this stressed out about sex."

That remark infuriated her further. "I am *not* stressed out about anything!"

"You are stressed out about everything." He smiled in a smug, obnoxious manner. "This rescue comes with no conditions—except that you have to relax. Since you don't want to use sex to do that, and since nothing else we've tried works, I suggest you find something that does. In the meantime, I'll keep looking for your mythical villain, if that's what you want. It won't work, though."

"What makes you so sure?" she challenged.

"Because it's impossible to find someone who doesn't exist."

9

IT WAS SEVEN O'CLOCK in the morning, and Chrissy was working in the flower bed.

Alec glowered at her through the dining-room window. She had on the respectable blouse-and-shorts outfit she'd been wearing when they arrived, and her hair was neatly coiled at the back. For some reason that increased his irritation with her.

He turned on a heel and stomped into the kitchen. He was heartily sick of watching Christine dig up the yard! Come to think of it, he was heartily sick of everything about her.

He opened a cupboard to pull out a mug and glared at the clean, organized contents. What was the matter with the woman, anyway? Why did she have to be so conscientious about everything? And what was the big deal about last night? He'd just suggested that they sleep together. There was nothing wrong with that. He'd only been trying to help—and she'd been just as aroused as he'd been! Couldn't she forget her involvement hang-up and simply enjoy life?

She'd told him that she didn't want to get involved with him in any way. What was her big objection? He might be irresponsible, lazy and unambitious, but apart from that, there wasn't anything wrong with him.

He might as well end this rescue. He wasn't very good at it. He couldn't find a killer who didn't exist, and he couldn't get Chrissy to calm down enough to realize one didn't.

He rested his bottom against the counter while he took a sip of his coffee. What would it take to convince her? He'd eliminated all the major suspects. Her brother didn't sound like a murderer, her competitors liked her and no one appeared to have a grudge against her.

You must have missed something.

Alec shook his head to clear away her words. He hadn't missed anything. She was wrong about that, too. He had worked very hard on this. It wasn't his fault no one was trying to kill her! Okay, there were a few loose ends lying around, and he wasn't exactly journalist of the year. But what else could he possibly do?

I think there was something...dangerous there.

Alec took another sip of his coffee and tried to push away a feeling of anxiety. That was impossible. There hadn't been anything dangerous on that golf course. No one knew where she was. Chrissy had just had some sort of "chronic compulsive memory" reaction, that's all. Although it was a little strange that she'd have it then. She hadn't seemed stressed out on that golf course. She'd been having a good time. Then...

He gave his head a shake. He'd better end this rescue before he got as paranoid as Christine.

He returned to the dining room and glanced out the window, suddenly anxious to see her again.

Her tools were there—the hoe, the spade, the rake. They were all where he'd seen them just a few minutes ago.

However, Christine was nowhere in sight.

NOW WHAT WAS SHE going to do?

Christine sat on the damp, spongy ground in the small grove of trees behind the house. She'd given up working in the garden. There just didn't seem to be any point. This rescue was over.

She rested her head back against the trunk of a tree and stared up at the branches. She hadn't slept at all last night. For one thing, she'd been scared to death that someone had found her. For another, she'd been absolutely and totally furious.

She didn't know who she was more mad at—Alec for being such a jerk or herself for being sucked in. She should have known better. She should have realized he'd never take this rescue seriously. She should have refused to come with him. Instead she'd let him take charge of her. She'd actually become attached to someone who didn't care about her at all. She'd been so stupid that she'd let him talk her into walking onto a golf course, thereby putting her life in danger. She'd only done it so she could get him to take her seriously. It had been a big waste of time. Alec hadn't taken one single thing about this mystery seriously. He'd just been playing amateur psychologist. He wanted her to admit she was nuts so he could stop feeling responsible. He'd even been willing to sleep with her to accomplish that.

Maybe he was right: maybe she was nuts. After all, her thumb had twitched yesterday and nothing had happened. Still, she was positive that feeling had meant something.

Now she was simply going to have to go back to work and hope she'd imagined the whole thing. If she hadn't...

She was so lost in thought that she didn't hear Alec approach until he spoke. "Christine?"

She glanced up. Alec was standing about two feet away from her. His face was almost perfectly white, and there were fresh coffee stains on his gray T-shirt. For a moment he just stared at her, while taking long, deep breaths. When he spoke, his voice sounded a little hoarse. "Are you, uh, all right?"

Christine had never felt less all right in her life. "I'm fine," she lied. She got to her feet and brushed the leaves and twigs off her shorts. "Why?"

"I, uh, just didn't know where you were." He raised a hand to rub the back of his neck. "I couldn't see you from the house and..." He blinked a couple of times and peered at his surroundings, as if seeing them for the first time. "What are you doing out here, anyway?"

Christine shrugged a shoulder. "I wasn't really doing anything. I just sort of...wandered out here to, uh, think."

"Think?" The expression on his face transformed into a dark scowl. "That's what you were doing here? Thinking?"

"That's right. I—"

"I almost had a heart attack and you were *thinking?*"

"A heart attack?" Now that he mentioned it, he didn't look all that healthy. His face, which had been so pale, was filling with color at an alarming rate, and there were white lines around the corners of his lips. "Has something happened or—"

"No, but it's about to." He compressed his lips and tightened his jaw, while his eyes narrowed with menace. "I'm going to do something I haven't done in years." He snaked out a hand and clamped his fingers around her wrist. "I'm going to lose my temper."

Then he did.

ALEC WAS STILL SHOUTING when they got back to the house.

Christine had yet to understand what had set him off. He'd marched back toward the house with her in tow, ranting all the while. Now they were in the kitchen, and he was still doing it. "There are eight goddamn rooms in this house," he snarled. "If you had an overwhelming need to think, you could have done it in one of them. There was no need to hide in the bushes to do it!"

Christine glowered at him across the expanse of kitchen floor while rubbing the wrist he'd recently released. She was getting very close to losing her own temper. She hadn't liked being dragged back here like a naughty child, and she didn't appreciate being yelled at, either, especially when she didn't understand the reason for it. "I was *not* hiding. I was just—"

"Or what about that garden you're so enamored with?" Alec made a large, exasperated gesture toward the window. "Couldn't you have thought in it? Or have you decided you don't want to get involved with it, either?"

Christine tightened her lips. "Is that what this is all about? You're mad because I won't fall into bed with you?"

Alec's eyes sparkled with warning. "No, Chrissy, that is *not* what this is about! This is about the fact that you—" he jabbed an accusing finger in her direction "—don't take this situation seriously."

Christine couldn't believe her ears. "*I* don't take it seriously?"

"No, you don't. You absolutely refuse to follow any of the rules." He listed off her crimes, using the fingers of one hand. "I told you to relax, and you didn't relax. I told you not to worry about our safety, and you kept worrying. I told you to tell me everything about yourself, and you didn't." His voice rose. "And I told you very specifically that you had to stay where I could see you, and you didn't do that, either!"

Right. She'd been out there crying because he didn't care about her. She was going to be sent back out into the world to be killed and all he could think about were his stupid rules. "Okay, maybe I didn't. But what difference does it make now? Your rules don't apply anymore, Alec. This rescue is over."

That just seemed to incite him further. "It is, is it? And who decided that?"

Christine stared into the angry green and blue of his eyes, startled by the question. Hadn't he decided that last night? "I thought... "

"You did, huh? And just when did you think that? When you were hiding out in the woods?"

"I was not..."

"Well, I've got news for you! It doesn't matter what *you* think. I'm the one who decides when this rescue is over! That's another rule that you seem to have conveniently forgotten!"

"I didn't forget it. I just..."

"You just what? Ignored it, like you did the rest?" He took an annoyed gulp of air. "Well, from now on you are going to follow the rules—and there are going to be severe penalties for breaking them, ones you won't like very much." He leaned back against the kitchen counter and folded his arms. "For instance, the penalty for 'hiding in the bushes to think' is that you are not allowed outside for the remainder of this rescue."

He couldn't be serious! "Oh, for heaven sakes, Alec, I'm not—"

"Yes, you are. You will stay inside. And if you don't—if you take one step out the door without an okay from me—I will lock you in the basement." He actually looked determined to do it, too. "It's impossible for me to accomplish anything if I have to waste all my time worrying about you!"

The kitchen settled into silence. Christine stared across the room at him while her mind analyzed that statement. "Worrying about me?" she echoed. "Is that why you're acting like this—because you were worried about me?"

"That's right!"

Christine blinked a couple of times. Now his behavior suddenly made sense. "But why would you be worried about me?" she wondered. "Don't you think the danger is all in my head?"

"I..." He clamped his lips together, then bent his head to examine his fingers. "I...don't know."

"You don't know? But last night..."

"Yeah, well, that was last night." His head came up, his expression mirroring the uncertainty in his voice. "This morning I—I wasn't so sure. When I looked out the window and realized you weren't there, I..." He drew in a breath. "I thought I might be wrong—that something had happened to you. I didn't think you'd leave that garden, considering it's the only thing around here you want to get involved with!"

Christine stood very still, while all the anger drained out of her. He'd been worried about her! He'd looked out that window, and she hadn't been there and he'd been worried about her! He'd rushed out to find her—to rescue her.

"Oh, Alec," she whispered. "That is so sweet." Then she was across the room, throwing herself against him. His arms tightened around her, and Christine hugged him fiercely, feeling him tremble as he held her. She had given him a scare, hadn't she? No wonder he'd been so cross.

And if he'd been that concerned about her, he must care something about her. Oh, he probably did still think she was a basket case, but he definitely cared.

She slipped a hand around his neck, pulled his head down to hers and kissed him passionately. Then she couldn't seem to get enough of him. She combed her fingers through his hair, and touched his face and stroked his shoulders, while pressing herself as close to him as she could get.

It wasn't enough. She wanted to be closer to him than this. She slipped her hands under his shirt and put her palms against his chest. The feel of him increased her desire. She wanted more. She wanted his bare skin under her cheek, to press her lips against his muscles, to touch him all over and... She grasped the hem of his shirt and began tugging it upward.

Alec captured her chin with a hand and held up her head to peer into her face. "Chrissy?"

Christine moistened her lips. She wasn't a person who got carried away with passion. She made informed, clear-headed decisions about things like this. But she did care for him, and he must care something for her. Besides, she wanted him more than she'd wanted anything for a long time.

She focused on his eyes, which revealed the same passion and need that she felt, and made her decision. "You're wrong, Alec," she whispered. "I'd much rather be involved with you than the garden." She yanked up his shirt and pressed herself against him in an attempt to make her meaning clear. "And if you're still interested in heavy breathing and hot sex, I think now might be a really good time to add it to this rescue."

SHE GOT HIS SHIRT OFF while they were still in the kitchen, thanks to Alec's cooperation. When she'd shoved it up to his shoulders, he shrugged it off, then took her in his arms. Christine fingered his back, then worked her way to the front, feeling her way down to the waistband of his shorts. She yanked those down, too. Alec made a sound that was half chuckle, half groan, and put his hands on hers to stop her. "Hang on, honey."

He helped her remove the rest of his clothes, and kicked them away. Christine ran her hand down his body, past the arrow of hair that trickled into a line, to close her fingers around his hard shaft. Alec groaned again and captured her wrist. "You'd better stop that or..."

Christine glanced up into his face. "But I want...I want..."

His grin was pure male satisfaction. "I know what you want, Chrissy, and I want it, too. But if you keep doing that, we won't make it out of the kitchen." He bent to swing her up into his arms. "I'm not sure I can walk in this condition, much less carry you, but now is a good time to find out."

Christine clung to his neck, kissing him wildly as he staggered up the stairs. He stumbled on the last few steps, but caught himself and made it to the top, leaning against the hall wall while he lowered her to the floor. "This is close enough," he decided. His hands roamed down her shoulders and arms. "Now what would you like to do?"

Christine hesitated, unsure of her next move. She didn't have much experience in this area. "I'm not sure. I haven't done this a lot and..."

Some of her uncertainty must have shown in her face, because Alec understood immediately. "It's okay, Chrissy. I can lead the way." He took her hand and drew her into his bedroom. "The first step is to get your clothes off."

Christine's fingers moved to her blouse and Alec shook his head. "No. I get to do that." He urged her over to the bed and tumbled them both down onto it, with her on top, then rolled so she was underneath him. The feel of his weight on her was as arousing as the feel of his bare skin. He kissed her ear, touched his tongue to her eyelids and swept his lips across hers. Then he eased himself lower, using his elbows to prop himself up, and began working on the buttons of her blouse.

It seemed to Christine that he took an hour to get her undressed. He'd expose a small patch of skin, stroke it with a finger, then use his lips and tongue on it before moving on. He finished with her blouse, then repeated the same exercise with her shorts, gliding them down over her hips, tasting and touching her every inch of the way. When his hands closed around her thighs, parting her legs for a wickedly intimate kiss, Christine quivered with pleasure and held out her arms for him. His weight came back fully on her. Then she was pushing him onto his back, eager to have the same taste of his body he'd had of hers.

She explored his chest with her mouth and her hands, pressing her lips against his chest, his abdomen, then finally cupping his manhood with her palm. She touched her tongue to him, and he groaned and shifted her aside. "One second, Chrissy." He sat up and yanked open the drawer in the bedside table. "The rescuer has to protect the rescuee—from everything."

He sheathed himself then stretched out beside her again, moved her legs apart and probed her intimately with his finger. Then he was on top of her again, gathering her to him, easing himself into her. Christine gasped with pleasure as she felt his body enter hers and he froze, holding himself above her on his elbows. "Okay?"

Her hands traveled over his face, then down to his shoulders. "Oh, yes."

"Me, too. You feel good, Chrissy. So good."

"So do you. So do you."

He smiled briefly, then raised her legs to wrap them around his and started moving against her in a slow, even pace that gradually increased with intensity until she was clutching him and gasping his name. "Alec, Alec, Alec."

"Right here with you." He gave one final hard thrust, and Christine shuddered with delicious tremors of pleasure.

He'd been right, she decided, as he groaned out his own release, then collapsed on top of her. This was one thing he handled very well.

"I GATHER YOU GOT OVER your aversion to becoming involved with me," Alec commented.

He angled his head so he could look down at Christine. She was sprawled in a contented heap across his chest, one of her arms curved around his waist, her cheek covered by her hair. His lips formed into a slow, triumphant smile. After all the blows she'd dealt to his ego, it had felt pretty good to have her practically ripping off his clothes. "Are you okay?" he asked.

"I'm better than okay," Christine murmured. "I'm..." she smiled briefly "...wonderful."

Alec grinned at the word. He was feeling pretty wonderful, too. He shifted her off him and rolled onto his side so he could see her face. Her eyes were half-open. He'd been right about them. They were very dark after making love. "I thought you didn't want to get involved with me." He put a hand on her face and stroked a thumb down her cheek. "What changed your mind? Are you turned on by men who shout at you or something?"

"That had nothing to do with it." Christine raised her head and brushed a light kiss across his jaw. "You were concerned about me and I...appreciated it."

Alec didn't believe that was her only reason for being in his bed. She'd said she had to be emotionally involved before she got physically involved. Well, they'd just been pretty physically involved. He figured it was safe to assume that they were emotionally involved as well.

The concept appealed to him. "I was more than

concerned," he said gruffly. "I was worried half to death. Don't you ever do anything like that again."

Her eyelids fluttered closed. "I won't."

She sounded content and compliant. Alec decided to take advantage of the situation. "And for the remainder of our time here, you'll follow all the rules?"

Christine's eyes popped open. "I thought this rescue was over." Alec opened his mouth and she put a finger on his lips to silence him. "Don't start yelling. I was just under the impression that you'd finished your investigation."

Alec closed his eyes while he marshaled his thoughts. Right now, his concern seemed like an overreaction. She hadn't been in any danger. Yet he had his doubts. "I thought I was, too," he admitted. He rolled onto his back and stared up at the white plaster ceiling. "However, after the way I felt this morning...well, I don't ever want to feel like that again. I want to be absolutely positive that you are going to be safe before you leave here. There are a few loose ends to clear up, and a few other things I should look into. And I want to go over everything I've done, just to make sure I haven't missed anything." He glanced sideways at her. "You're going to have to stay here for a few more days. I'm not quite finished rescuing you yet."

"Oh." Christine's cheeks flooded with color. "Well, I don't have to be anywhere for a couple more days.

And there isn't another rescuer in sight, so I guess you can have a few more days to finish rescuing me."

"Good." He snuggled her close. "But this time you have to follow all the rules."

"Every single one," she promised. "At least, all the ones I can remember." She rolled on top of him. "But this time, you'd better do it right."

"What?"

She gazed down at him, and the gray in her eyes got darker and deeper and dreamier. "From now on, this rescue has to include a lot of heavy breathing and hot sex."

Alec chuckled and raised her so he could close his lips around one of her breasts. "I think that can be arranged."

10

"ALL RIGHT," Christine conceded the next afternoon. "I give up. The world is right, and I'm crazy." She tossed the notebook onto the dining-room table and got to her feet. "Now can I stop doing this?"

Alec barely looked up from his computer screen. "Nope."

"But we've been at this all day. I'm not accomplishing anything. I can't think of anything or anyone you've missed." She looked longingly out the window. The sun was shining brightly, there wasn't a cloud in the sky and her gardening tools were right where she'd left them yesterday when she'd wandered off into the trees. There was still a lot of work to do out there. "Maybe if I had a little fresh air..."

Alec raised his head long enough to frown across the table at her. "Absolutely not! You're not allowed outside today, Chrissy. That's your penalty for breaking a rule yesterday and scaring me half to death. I thought I told you that."

He had shouted something like that at her, but Christine thought it had been settled. "You're not still mad at me about that, are you?"

Alec stroked a palm across his chin while he considered it. "I wouldn't say I was mad about it." He studied her with a warm, possessive gaze. "If we weren't involved, I would be, but since we are, I'm not."

Christine cupped a hand across her mouth to hide her smile. Alec seemed to be quite taken with the idea of being "involved." He'd mentioned the word at least five times today. She took another look out the window. "Well, since you're not still mad about it, and since I already apologized, I would think—"

Alec held up a hand. "Apologies don't help. Once a penalty has been assigned, it can't be unassigned." He lifted his shoulders in a helpless shrug. "I can't change it. It's just one of the rules. And I'd hate to have to lock you in the basement." He gestured toward the notebook. "Just go through the list one more time, okay? You might think of something you forgot to tell me." He paused meaningfully. "Or someone you forgot to tell me about."

Christine sighed, picked up the notebook and pretended to read it while watching Alec from under the cover of her lashes. He had on one of his usual ripped shirt-and-track-short combinations, and although he had shaved—for her benefit, she suspected—his hair had been carelessly combed with his fingers, and he looked as wild and disreputable as ever. His light-hearted air was firmly in place, enhanced by a self-satisfied curve of his lips whenever he looked at her.

Under different circumstances Christine would have found that irritating, but today she didn't—probably because she was sure she had the exact same expression on her face. He'd promised her heavy breathing and hot sex, and he'd certainly provided it. If she'd realized that was what it would be like to be with him, she would have crawled into his bed a lot sooner.

She flushed at the thought and focused back on the notebook. Today she couldn't complain that Alec wasn't applying himself to his task. He'd been working hard all day, reading through his notes and forcing her to go through them. He'd been sending E-mail on his computer, faxing people and talking to others on the phone, confirming all his information, dredging up more "suspects" to add to his list—all of whom were a small possibility at best. It was certainly commendable, and very touching...and almost as infuriating as when he hadn't been taking it seriously!

Christine scolded herself for her attitude. Now that he was taking the task to heart, she didn't seem to be. She felt as if a load had been lifted off her shoulders. Besides, she was too enamored with the way his hair fell into his eyes, with his profile when he turned his head, the curve of his fingers around the receiver. She kept thinking about the feel of his skin under her palms and the way his mouth felt on...

She gave her head a little shake to clear it. Obviously all that heavy breathing and hot sex had affected her brain. She really should make more of an effort to include it in her life every so often. That wasn't going to be easy, considering her schedule. Of course, she could always rearrange things—make a few adjustments so she could see Alec....

She tightened her lips at the thought. What was the matter with her? She wasn't going to change her schedule! When this rescue ended, their relationship would end, the way her others had. She'd be busy with her job and these feelings would dissipate. As for Alec, well, his feelings for her were all wrapped up in a genuine concern for her welfare, along with a strong feeling of responsibility. As soon as this rescue was over, both of those would be gone. He'd go back to his life of fun, fun, fun, and she'd go back to hocking bean curd. The idea made her feel a little ill.

She thumbed through his notes again. There was something she hadn't told him about—and someone. The someone was Estelle and the something was her twitching thumb. Alec might just end the whole thing if he found out that Christine relied on her thumb to warn her of danger—and she wasn't ready for their time together to be over. She pushed herself abruptly to her feet. "Am I allowed to leave the room to make supper? Or will you lock me in the basement for that, too?"

"Well..." Alec pondered the question. "That all depends. What are you planning on making?" His eyes narrowed suspiciously. "And what color is it?"

"I THINK IT'S pretty safe to cross Keith off the suspect list," Alec announced that evening.

He eased his feet up onto the footstool and slid an arm around Christine, who was nestled on the couch beside him. Alec pressed his lips against her temple before continuing, smiling as he noted that she didn't back away. Apparently now that they were involved, he could touch her and kiss her as much as he wanted.

The idea pleased him. This involvement stuff wasn't bad at all. The only thing wrong with it was that it had increased his feeling of protectiveness and added a new element of possessiveness. Even those weren't *bad* feelings. And he certainly liked the thought of having her in his bed for more than two hours. Making love with her hadn't diminished his desire. As a matter of fact, it had increased it. He'd enjoyed having her spend most of the day in the dining room with him, but it had made it difficult to concentrate. Having her curled up beside him, reading his notes over his shoulder, with one of her hands resting on his thigh, was having the same effect.

He gave his head a shake and referred back to his notebook. "What was I saying? Oh, yeah, Keith. I've confirmed that he's in Europe, I've investigated his financial situation, and he just doesn't seem to have any sort of a motive to want to hurt you." He tapped his pencil thoughtfully against the page. "He could have some deep sibling-rivalry thing, I suppose, but..."

"I don't think so. Keith wouldn't want to hurt me."

Alec couldn't imagine anyone wanting to hurt her, but he wasn't jumping to any conclusions this time. He scanned his notes again. "I'm still looking into HoleSum's competition. This Robert Shultzer guy seems to be our best bet. I've got some friends of mine doing a thorough check on him. And I'm still looking into your former competitors. There is the possibility that one of them is carrying a grudge." It was a slim possibility, but Alec wasn't going to pass up anything. He paused for a moment. "And I've also eliminated those two other guys you were 'involved' with."

Christine's head came up. "You...talked to them?"

"I thought I should. If I'm going to do a thorough job of this, I have to look in every corner." That wasn't the only reason he'd called them, though. He'd suddenly been quite curious about them, although he wasn't sure why.

"Yes, but..." Chrissy's cheeks colored. "I'm sure they aren't trying to kill me."

"So am I. They sounded much too dull to do anything like that." He put a hand over his mouth and faked a yawn. "A lawyer and an accountant. What did you see in those guys?"

"Well..." Christine's expression suggested she

wasn't sure, either. "They were nice enough, I suppose...."

"*Nice?*" Alec shuddered at the word. Was that what she was going to say about him someday?

Christine ran her tongue along her bottom lip. "What did they say?"

"About you, you mean?" Alec didn't have to refer to his notes for this. He rested his head back, closed his eyes and recited from memory. "Well, according to them, you were a charming, pleasant companion and they regretted that you were no longer part of their lives."

"Oh."

Alec raised his eyelids slightly to look down at her. "So why aren't you? Part of their lives, I mean. Did they do something, or..."

"Oh, no." Christine shook her head. "It wasn't anything like that. They were fine. I was just busy with my job and—"

"Your job!" He should have guessed. "Is that really all you care about—your job? Don't you want a husband and a picket fence and a thirty-six-inch television screen like everyone else?"

"Well, uh, I suppose at some time I wouldn't mind that." She eyed him curiously. "What about you? Is that what you want?"

Alec tapped his pencil against his bottom lip. "I haven't given it much thought." Of course, he'd never been involved before, either. Hell, he'd never even lived with a woman for longer than a weekend before. Now that he'd done it, maybe it was time he thought about other things, too. "I suppose I wouldn't mind a football team of little Alecs running around." He considered it for a moment, then pushed the thought aside. "But first I've got to finish rescuing you." He rubbed his eyes. "Can you think of anything or anyone I've missed?"

Christine averted her eyes and shook her head. "No."

Alec heaved a huge mental sigh. Christine had yet to tell him about Estelle. He hadn't mentioned it. He figured if Chrissy knew he'd talked to her friend, she might be angry enough to call the whole thing off. Not only did he not want their little arrangement to end just yet, he also didn't like the idea of her going back out into the public before they were absolutely sure it would be safe. He kissed her hair again, then regretfully pushed himself to his feet. "I've got some more phone calls to make. If anything crosses your mind, let me know."

CHRISTINE SAT in the living room, listening to the distant sound of Alec's voice as he talked on the phone and feeling guiltier and guiltier by the second. He'd worked hard all day and he didn't show any signs of stopping. She was starting to get a little concerned about him. Heavens, he'd even eaten his vegetables this evening without a single comment. Serious was *not* good for him.

She turned the page of the book she was trying to read, then tossed it onto the table. Alec's earlier questions had bothered her, too. She'd never found the idea of settling down particularly appealing. Now she realized she wouldn't mind having a house and a yard of her own—and someone like Alec around. However, that wasn't even an option, with her current life-style.

She considered his comments. A football team of little Alecs was exactly what he should have. And there would probably be some sexy woman in there somewhere, as well.

The idea bothered her a lot. She pushed herself to her feet. Maybe it was time she told him everything. After all, he didn't seem to have missed anything. Perhaps she did have this compulsive-memory thing. Even if that wasn't the problem, she had a feeling she'd better end this rescue, before she got any more attached to Alec.

She wandered into the dining room and stood in the door. "Alec?"

He glanced up. "Hmm?"

"There's something I should tell you. But you have to promise not to say anything until I finish."

Alec's forehead furrowed. "Does it have anything to do with...sports psychology?"

"No." She moistened her lips. "It has something to do with, uh, thumbs."

"YOUR THUMB TWITCHED?" Alec echoed.

He was sitting on the sofa, with his legs spread wide and his forearms resting on his knees. He stared at her with blue-green eyes that looked more surprised than amused. "You were walking across this parking lot and your thumb started to twitch?"

"That's right." Christine sank into a chair across from him. "It was a strange feeling. First my heart rate increased. Then I started to feel...frightened. It was dark, I was alone. Then I heard a car coming. I jumped to one side and it zipped right across the parking lot..." She shuddered. "Right where I'd been standing."

Alec blinked twice.

"That's why I thought the car was aiming for me." She sighed. "I didn't know what to make of it. I called my friend, Dr. Estelle Lamont. She suggested that it was just an accident, and that I was suffering from some sort of chronic compulsive memory syndrome that was making me respond in a paranoid fashion." Christine gave her head a quick side-to-side shake. "I didn't really believe Estelle's theory, but I didn't have any other explanation. Then it happened again."

"The hotel room?" Alec guessed.

"That's right. I put the key in the lock, and my thumb started to twitch. When I opened the door, there was a man there. I didn't get a good look at him, but...I was terrified."

Alec shoved one hand through his hair. "Let me guess. The same thing happened in Colorado."

"That's right," Christine admitted. "My thumb started twitching when I left my hotel to go to that charity thing. By the time that gun went off, I was a nervous wreck. I was positive it had been meant for me."

Alec laced his fingers together and studied them, while taking several long, deep breaths.

Christine took a deep breath herself and went on. "Then at Keith's cottage—just before the fire—it happened again. That's why I left."

Alec didn't say anything. Christine was suddenly very sorry she'd told him about it. This was Alec O'Brian, after all. He could write a little story about this that would ruin her career, her reputation and the rest of her life. "Look," she said. "I—I know how crazy this sounds. I—"

"You're right, Chrissy," Alec agreed. "It does sound crazy." His head came up, the blue in his eyes more vivid than ever. "As a matter of fact, it is the craziest thing I have heard in my entire life!" He sprang to his feet. "When you think your life is in danger you do *not* go play a round of golf!"

Christine's jaw dropped as she took in his expression. His mouth was a straight line, his eyebrows were lowered, and he looked almost as angry as he had yesterday. "I had to play," she explained. "HoleSum was sponsoring—"

"HoleSum was sponsoring it? That's a good reason to risk your life?"

"I didn't know..."

"You had reason to suspect! Did you ask them to beef up security? No! Did you announce that you were coming down with the flu and needed to rest? No! You just waltzed out there!" He shook his head. "Either you are the bravest person I've ever met or you're the dumbest!"

This was not quite the reaction she had been expecting. "I, uh..."

Alec paced over to the window, rubbed his hand along the back of his neck, then turned to face her. "Just a minute. Yesterday, on the golf course..."

"That's right," Christine admitted. "It happened again. That's why I insisted that we leave. There didn't seem to be anyone around, and the twitching stopped almost immediately. But when we got back here and you started to come in...well, I thought someone may have been here and I..."

"Ah, for crissakes!" He rolled his eyes toward the ceiling, then looked back at her. "You pushed me aside in case it wasn't safe in here. Is that it?"

Christine nodded. "I was just checking. I wanted to see if something was wrong in the cottage first." She shook her head. "There wasn't—but I still thought it meant someone had been here. Maybe it didn't."

Alec swore liberally and took the necessary steps to cross the distance between them. He clamped his hands around her arms and pulled her to her feet, his face a study in annoyance. "Don't you ever do anything like that again!"

"Alec..."

"I am your rescuer, lady! I protect you, not the other way around!" His face lost its color. "What if you'd been right? What if someone had been in here? You..."

He kept on talking but Christine wasn't listening. She was swallowing around the enormous lump in her throat. He wasn't making fun of her, after all! He believed her, and he was taking her seriously!

"All right," she admitted. "I guess I did break another rule."

"You're darn right you did," Alec grumbled. He took his hands off her arms, rested them against the back of the chair and leaned his weight onto them, looming over her. "And you..."

Christine slipped a hand around his neck and stroked her fingers into his hair. "I suppose there's a severe penalty for doing that."

"You bet there is." Alec hissed in a breath as she nibbled on his earlobe. "That's against the rules, too," he growled. "The rescuee is not allowed to distract the rescuer when he's assigning penalties." He groaned as she slipped a caressing hand around his shoulders, then down into the waistband of his shorts. "Oh, hell," he said. "I think assigning penalties can wait for a little while."

"AND IF ANYTHING on your body twitches, I want to know about it," Alec concluded.

He glanced down to see how his lecture was being received. Christine didn't look too fascinated. She had one elbow propped on his rib cage, her forehead furrowed in a concentrated expression. However, what she seemed to be concentrating on was not his lecture. She seemed much more fascinated by the lazy circles she was drawing with a finger on his chest. "When the rescuer is giving a lecture, the rescuee is supposed to be paying attention," Alec admonished.

"Oh?" Christine bent her head and stroked her tongue erotically across his nipple. "What's the penalty for ignoring him completely?"

Alec almost groaned out loud at the rush of pleasure her touch created. He hooked a finger under her chin to raise her head, and found himself looking into two very dark gray eyes. Chrissy had something on her mind, but he didn't think it had anything to do with rescues—unless it was the heavy-breathing-and-hot-sex part.

Not that he didn't have that on his mind as well. Chrissy had to be the most sensuous, responsive woman he'd ever been with. How could a person like her go a whole year without a relationship?

He realized where this train of thought was leading and sighed. If they spent all day in bed, he'd never finish his job. "I'm serious, Chrissy."

She nipped at his finger with her teeth. "Maybe you shouldn't be serious."

He angled his head so he could see her face. "What?"

"I don't know if there's anything to be serious about." She sighed and rolled off him, onto her back. "Yesterday, my thumb twitched and nothing happened."

Alec felt his lips form into a frown. "So?"

"I thought my twitching thumb was an indication that something horrible was about to happen. But maybe that isn't always the case. I'm positive it was in Keith's cabin. But those other times...well, I don't know. Maybe it is all coincidence and...some chronic-compulsive-memory thing like Estelle suggested." She clasped a hand over her mouth and gazed guiltily at Alec.

Alec stared up at the ceiling, pretending not to notice her expression. "Estelle told *me* it was all related to former stress—golf courses, grass, crowds...."

Christine rose up on an elbow to look down into his face. "You've talked to her?"

"Uh-huh." He grinned at her surprise. "I'm a pretty decent reporter. I managed to track her down." He reached out to give her bottom an admonishing squeeze. "That's another rule you've broken. You were supposed to tell me everything."

"I know, but..." She was still staring at him in amazement. "I thought if you heard her theories, you'd write me off as a nutcase." Her brow furrowed. "Why didn't you tell me you'd talked to her?"

Alec shrugged. "I didn't see the point. I know she believes you need to go to the Lamont Clinic for some sort of relaxation therapy, but I don't." He rubbed a palm up and down her back. "You seem to be relaxing just fine here."

"Sex therapy for the crazy lady," Christine teased. She kissed the corner of Alec's mouth. "Maybe that *is* all I needed. After all, no one could have been at that golf course. No one knows where I am."

Alec closed his eyes while he considered that. It was the most logical explanation, and it was the theory he'd had in the first place—that Chrissy's problems were all due to stress. Still, the whole thing gave him the creeps. "Let's not jump to any conclusions," he advised. "I've still got a few more people to check out."

He held Chrissy close, feeling more possessive and protective than ever.

This rescue was all out of whack. She was relaxing, and he'd never felt more tense in his life.

11

ALEC WASN'T FEELING any less uptight the next morning. He'd risen early, made a number of calls, talked to practically everyone he could think of, and he still didn't know much more than when he'd started.

He wandered into the kitchen, slumped down in a chair and watched Christine fuss around with a bunch of odd-looking ingredients on the kitchen counter. She was wearing his green T-shirt, which reached her knees; she had bare feet; her hair was loosely tied back with a shoelace. She sure didn't look like a stressed-out basket case to him.

Of course, he hadn't exactly found a villain, either.

"What are you making?" he asked with little interest.

"A...candy-bar-and-ice-cream casserole."

"Yeah?" Alec raised his head. "What color is it?"

"Orange."

"Orange sounds awfully healthy," he complained.

Christine gave his shoulder a bracing pat as she passed. "Cheer up. In a couple of days you'll be able to eat all the junk food you want."

The idea made Alec's stomach a little queasy. She was right. Once this mission ended, he was going to be back to eating whatever he wanted. He'd be hanging out in bars and watching sports, writing meaningless articles no one cared about, having meaningless sex with someone he wasn't involved with and—

Christine's voice interrupted his thoughts. "Did you find out...anything?"

"Nothing useful," Alec admitted. "I called the golf course. All the other people there at the same time as us were locals." He paused. "I talked to them all and none of them recall seeing anything out of the ordinary."

"Oh." Christine's shoulders drooped. She blinked rapidly and turned to busy herself with the casserole.

Alec sensed her despondent mood and sighed. He didn't feel all that pleased about the results, either, but he shouldn't have been surprised. This twitching-thumb thing was probably more stress related than danger related. Probably.

Christine glanced over her shoulder at him. "Anything else?"

"Well...I did do a check on that doctor friend of yours."

"Estelle?" Christine shook her head. "Estelle has nothing to do with this."

"Probably not," Alec agreed. "She is a bit...bizarre, though." He tilted his head to one side and admired the view of Christine from the back. "How did you get mixed up with her, anyway?"

"I met her years ago. She was doing some sort of physiological testing on athletes and a bunch of us volunteered. She and I have been friends ever since."

"She's not much of a friend if she goes around telling people you've got this compulsive-chronic-memory thing." Alec pushed himself out of the chair and wandered over to open the fridge. "That clinic of hers isn't doing too well, you know. Apparently her federal funding is going to be canceled in September. If you'd left all your money to it, then she'd be a great suspect. As it is, I don't think your death would help much."

"It wouldn't." Christine wrinkled her nose. "I didn't know Estelle's clinic had financial problems." She considered it for a moment. "I guess I'm not all that surprised. Estelle is a really nice person, but her ideas can be a bit odd. The last time I was talking to her, I..."

Alec paused in the midst of drinking milk out of the carton and glanced over at her. Her eyes were wide and round, her bottom lip was tucked under her front teeth and there was a faint flush on her cheeks. "Go on," he encouraged her. "The last time you were talking to her, you what?"

She wiped her hands on her apron, taking great care not to meet his eyes. "It's, uh...nothing. At least, I'm pretty sure it's nothing."

Alec had a strong suspicion it was something. He

replaced the milk carton in the fridge. "I'm the boss here. I decide what's important and what isn't."

"Yes, well..." Christine sighed and her lips curved into a tiny, apologetic smile. "It's just that...well, the last time I was talking to Estelle, I did mention something that maybe I shouldn't have."

"Oh?" Alec didn't understand Chrissy's reticence. "Like what?" He shoved the fridge door closed and leaned back against it. "When was the last time you were talking to Estelle?"

"A couple of days ago."

Alec shook his head. "You couldn't have. You've been here..." He suddenly got it. "Oh, for God's sake, Chrissy, you didn't tell her about our setup, did you?"

"Of course not!" She drew in a deep breath. "But I do think I might have mentioned...Cremona."

THAT DID IT, Alec decided. The second this rescue was over, he was registering Christine in a course for the rescue challenged.

He sat in a chair in the dining room, listening to Chrissy talk on the phone and mentally reviewing the penalty that was going to be associated with this latest breach of protocol.

Actually, he didn't think it mattered all that much—unless Estelle had mentioned Cremona to someone else.

Which was the reason for this phone call.

"That's right," Christine was saying. "I'm with Alec O'Brian.... Yes, I know what I said about him, but I was wrong. He's actually, um...wonderful." She gave Alec a small, hopeful smile that was not going to get her off the hook. "He's, uh, rescuing me."

Alec carefully monitored the conversation. It had been Christine's idea to call Estelle and ask if she'd mentioned Cremona to anyone. Alec hadn't been positive it was a wise idea, but it was the only lead they had. Besides, he'd already eliminated Estelle as a suspect.

"You didn't?" Christine's shoulders drooped. She met Alec's gaze and shook her head. "You're positive...? Okay. Thank you... No, I can't tell you that. It's, uh, against the rules. Yes. Yes, I know what you think, but no... I have to go now, Estelle. Goodbye." She replaced the receiver, leaned back in the chair and heaved an enormous sigh. "So much for that theory."

Alec's annoyance with her immediately faded, replaced by concern. "She's positive?"

"Absolutely." Christine sighed again and made a derisive face as she met his gaze. "She insists that I've got this compulsive-chronic-memory thing. I thought it was just another one of her weird theories. She's been trying for years to find someone who has it." She bent her head and bit her lip. "It looks as if she just did."

"We don't know that for sure," Alec muttered, although he was inclined to agree with her.

Christine raised her chin and tucked an errant strand of hair behind her ear. "There isn't any other conclusion to come to, Alec. You said you were at a dead end. We don't have any suspects left."

Alec shifted uncomfortably. That was true, too. "There are still a few people I could—"

"I've seen that list." Christine sank into a chair. "They're all former competitors I've beaten, or someone who once said I was 'intense'...." She shook her head. "They are *not* good suspects."

"Maybe not, but I'm still not one hundred percent convinced." He picked up her left hand and stroked a finger along her thumb. "This thumb thing has me worried. If it hadn't been for it, you could very well have been burned up in that fire."

"That could have been a—a coincidence."

It probably was, but Alec was still uncomfortable with it. He peered into her face. "Do you really believe that?"

Her eyes met his, then lowered. "I don't know what to think." Her lips moved in a pale imitation of a smile. "I suppose I'll find out when I get back to work. If I live through my next few public appearances, I guess I can safely assume that I just needed a little R and R."

For years he'd been taking potshots at her in his column, suggesting that she couldn't handle pressure. Now she was calmly talking about walking out in front of a crowd and making herself a target. "You can forget that," Alec advised gruffly. "Rescues aren't over until the rescuer says they're over. That means you aren't going to put yourself at risk until I am convinced it's safe."

"I don't have any choice, Alec. It's my job. I have responsibilities...."

Alec felt a surge of resentment against this stupid job of hers. "You're not going to risk your life for health food."

"What else can I do? I can't stay here and let you protect me forever...." Her teeth touched her bottom lip, and her eyes suddenly sparkled with excitement. "I know what I can do. I can go back to that golf course."

"YOU ARE BEING completely unreasonable," Christine complained.

She plopped down on one of the chairs in the dining room and glared at Alec, feeling the familiar combination of exasperation and admiration. He was sprawled in a chair across from her, his legs stretched out in front of him. He had shaved, but his hair had been combed carelessly. He had on a gray T-shirt and a pair of black shorts. His feet were bare, and just looking at him was so distracting she could hardly concentrate on the conversation.

"It doesn't matter if I'm unreasonable," he explained. "I'm in control around here. I get to make all the decisions and you get to do as you're told. I believe that's rule number three." His brow furrowed in a quizzical expression. "Or maybe it's rule number four."

"It's probably rule number four thousand," Christine muttered. "And I don't care what rule it is! I am making a perfectly rational suggestion...."

"That's your idea of a rational suggestion?" Alec shook his head emphatically. "When you think someone is trying to kill you, you don't go play a round of golf!"

"I did a couple of days ago," Christine reminded him.

"I thought it was safe then," Alec countered. "Now I'm not so sure."

"I am!" Christine insisted. "Come on, Alec, be reasonable. You've done a great job of looking into this, but you haven't found anyone with any sort of a motive to hurt me! The other day my thumb twitched and nothing happened. Therefore it's logical to conclude that I have just had a few unlucky accidents, and I'm not in any danger."

"Or we could also conclude that someone is hovering around, looking for you."

Christine shivered at that. "You checked out everything, and no one was there. And even if there is someone, I can't think of a better way to flush that person out."

Alec glanced over at her, narrowed his eyes and set his jaw. "Forget it, Chrissy. The damsel in distress does not act as bait. And you aren't going to that golf course or anyplace else until I'm convinced it's safe."

"When will that be?" Christine demanded. "I've got to be at a store opening—"

"It'll open just fine without you."

"But—"

Alec captured the back of her neck with one hand and gave her a swift kiss. "Arguing with me is against the rules," he reminded her when he raised his head. "That was the penalty."

Christine glowered at him. "You can't keep distracting me by kissing me."

"Count yourself lucky. I could have come up with a worse penalty." His eyes glinted wickedly. "For example, I could have said that the penalty for arguing is that we make love right here on the dining-room table."

Christine couldn't believe he would actually suggest that! "It's a good thing you didn't, because I would never do anything like that."

He arched an eyebrow. "Why not?"

"I just... I mean..." A mental image of them doing that flashed through her mind. Her mouth went dry and her heart pounded with excitement at the idea. "Well, for goodness sakes, Alec, it's the dining room and..."

He got to his feet, slid a hand under her knees and

picked her up. "There's nothing wrong with the dining room. As a matter of fact, I think one of the requirements of a rescue is that the rescuer and the rescuee make love in the dining room at least once during a rescue."

"We can't…"

He set her on the table and nuzzled his head into her neck, holding her with one hand while the other lowered the zipper on her shorts. "Are you arguing about it?" he asked as his fingers slipped inside her panties.

Suddenly this seemed like a really good idea. She thought fleetingly that she wouldn't have much chance to do something like this again for a long time.

He put an arm around her waist, lifted her and began tugging down her shorts. Christine rested her head against him. "I am definitely arguing about it," she whispered into his ear.

12

"I WONDER WHAT the penalty for this is?" Christine mumbled to herself as she steered Alec's car down the highway the next morning.

Alec hadn't specifically said that "borrowing" his car and heading for the forbidden golf course was against the rules. However, she had a strong suspicion that it was. She just hoped the penalty had more to do with heavy breathing and hot sex than it did with being locked in a basement.

She also hoped she lived to find out what the penalty was.

"Oh, don't be so paranoid, Christine," she told herself out loud. "Alec is being stubborn, that's all. This is a perfectly safe thing to do."

Even if it wasn't, she had to do it. Tomorrow, no matter what Alec said, this rescue was going to be over. She was going to have to get up in public and act like the cool, controlled, respectable representative of HoleSum Foods. She couldn't fake that if she thought someone was trying to kill her.

She also had to find some way to convince Alec to end their arrangement. Unless he believed she was in no danger, he'd never stop feeling responsible for her. Tomorrow she simply had to be at that store opening. Her job, her social programs, everything depended on it. There were only two ways to end it. Either they identified the villain, or they both agreed that she had some sort of stress problem. This was the quickest and surest way to accomplish that.

All she had to do was play the course. If there was a killer lurking around, he should show up pretty quickly. Her thumb would twitch, she'd get out of sight, and if she was lucky, she'd see someone or something. If she didn't, she'd keep on playing. And if her thumb didn't twitch at all, well, at least she'd know she didn't have some weird sort of phobia— and surely she could conclude that she'd never been in any danger. Then Alec would stop feeling responsible, and she'd get on with her life—and back to her job.

The idea held little appeal. Christine tried to argue herself out of it. She enjoyed her work, some parts of it anyway. She told herself that as soon as she was back at it, she'd forget all about her time with Alec.

She parked the car in the parking lot of the Cremona golf course. It was six o'clock in the morning, and there wasn't another soul around. It looked safe enough.

She took a deep breath of the cool morning air and climbed out of the car.

ALEC SNATCHED UP the phone on the first ring. "Chrissy?"

Christine's voice practically gurgled out of the receiver. "I did it, Alec! I did it! I played the whole course and nothing even remotely interesting happened."

Alec let out a breath he'd been holding ever since he'd woken up and found Christine gone, her disappearance explained by a note. "Thank God."

"I even played well," Christine burbled. "I think it's all that hot sex and heavy breathing. You know, I'm going to try to include a section on that in my next workshop."

Alec's stomach, which had stopped churning, started again. "Get back here, Chrissy."

"I don't know," she teased. "Exactly how angry with me are you?"

He was definitely pissed off at her, but right now he just wanted to have her back safe and sound. "I'm not all that thrilled, but—"

"I had to do it! I had to find out what would happen! And nothing did! I think I can assume that nothing happened there before! I must have just been stressed out or something!" She giggled again. "No one is trying to kill me! I'm just nuts! Now I can get back to work without worrying, and you can stop feeling responsible."

Every muscle in Alec's body clenched at her words. "Christine..."

"I'm on my way. But no locking me in the basement, okay?"

"No deal," Alec growled. He slowly replaced the receiver. Maybe he *should* lock her in the basement. That way she wouldn't go haring off to that stupid job of hers.

He got to his feet and paced around the room. He shouldn't be feeling this way. His rescue was going to turn out more or less the way he'd planned. Chrissy was no longer a nervous wreck. She'd relaxed, and was now convinced that her life was in no danger. Her attitude toward him had changed, and they'd spent some very pleasant days together. He should be feeling pretty darn pleased with himself.

However, pleased was not the emotion Alec was feeling. He was tense and irritable, and he had an almost irresistible desire to blow up every single HoleSum Foods store in existence. Is that really how she saw this mission ending—with a round of golf, and then she'd just go back to hocking alfalfa sprouts? What about him? Weren't they involved? Maybe he didn't know much about involvement, but he was positive it didn't have anything to do with alfalfa sprouts.

Besides, rescues weren't supposed to end this way. They were supposed to end with people living happily ever after...or perishing in the attempt to do so.

That thought caused his entire body to break out in goose bumps. He took several deep breaths and tried to reassure himself. No one was going to perish. He'd checked out all the suspects, and he hadn't found a single one with any decent motive to bump off Chrissy.

Had he missed anything?

He wandered into the dining room and picked up his notepad. Motive, means and opportunity. Keith might have the means and opportunity, but he really didn't have a motive, after all. HoleSum's competition was still a question mark, but it was a tiny one. Any former competitors who had a grudge had been checked out. Besides, if Chrissy's thumb meant anything, then someone had to have been at that golf course the other day. That was impossible. No one knew she was anywhere around here except for Estelle, and she hadn't told anyone. She certainly didn't have a motive herself. As a matter of fact, Estelle would be a lot better off if Chrissy was alive and suffering from this memory thing Estelle was so keen on....

Alec paused at the thought. As a matter of fact, Estelle would be an awful lot better off if Chrissy did have this chronic memory syndrome. Her research funding would be restored. There would be a great deal of publicity from the whole thing—probably a book, a made-for-TV movie—and all that media coverage would have thousands of people flocking to the Lamont Clinic, thinking they were all stressed out from looking at a tree leaf or something.

Was he the one being paranoid here? Or was it one hell of an enormous coincidence that the first person in the universe to have this chronic-memory thing happened to be friends with the psychiatrist who'd thought it up in the first place?

It seemed incredibly improbable and totally ridiculous. Still, he hadn't found anyone who would benefit from Chrissy's demise. But he had just found someone who would benefit from her being driven just a little crazy.

And yesterday Chrissy had told that someone all about this rescue—and who she was staying with.

It wouldn't be difficult to track Alec down, if someone had narrowed the search to Cremona. Maybe Chrissy had been perfectly safe on that golf course because the villain had a better place to look for her now.

Alec heard the sound of a car engine and jumped to his feet. Chrissy must be home. Now his mission was back on track. He'd deduced a villain. He could get the "damsel in distress" away from here, put together his information, talk it over with the police....

He rushed to the door, pulled it open and froze. It wasn't his car that had pulled up in front of the house. It was a gray sedan. And it wasn't Chrissy who was getting out of it, either.

MAYBE SHE WASN'T CURED.

Christine slowed to take the turn down the lane toward the house. The place looked exactly the same as it had when she'd left—sunlight sparkling on the windows, the yard looking a lot better than when she'd arrived.

But darn it, that stupid thumb of hers had started twitching again. "Golf course," Christine whispered to herself. "Stress. Stuff like that." There wasn't anything dangerous in there—except a rather grumpy rescuer with some naughty sort of penalty on his mind.

So why was she feeling so uneasy?

She hadn't been uneasy on the course. She hadn't even been uneasy in the parking lot. She'd actually been singing when she'd left—and looking forward to one more day with Alec. They wouldn't have to worry about following clues and looking for mythical murderers. She could spend the rest of the day with him before she turned back into the respectable HoleSum Foods lady.

Why was she having a panic attack now?

She parked the car beside the house and slowly climbed out. As she did, the front door opened. However, it wasn't Alec who emerged. It was a short, dark-haired woman dressed in a blue business suit.

Christine stared at her in stunned amazement, then let her breath out in a relieved sigh and hurried across the lawn toward her friend. "Estelle!" she exclaimed. "What on earth are you doing here?"

"AND WHEN I REALIZED what was going on, I knew I was simply going to have to come in person," Estelle explained. "I would have come before, but..."

"That's...very sweet of you," Christine murmured. "But you didn't have to bother. I'm fine. Really." She took an apprehensive look around. She didn't feel all that fine. She was tense and nervous, and unaccountably frightened. There didn't seem to be anything to be frightened about, though. Estelle had just come out of the house, and she was okay.

Christine studied her friend. "How did you get here, Estelle? There's no car...."

"Oh, uh, George brought me. He's a...colleague of mine. He's just left to run an errand."

"Oh." Christine took a couple of deep breaths and told herself her feelings were irrational. "Well." She swung open the front door. "Let's go inside then. I'm sure you've met Alec...." That's who she wanted to see, Christine decided. She was suddenly very desperate to see Alec.

"I've met him, yes."

"Well, where is he?" Christine hurried down the hall and into the living room, fully expecting to see Alec sprawled in his usual fashion on the sofa. But he wasn't there. "Alec?" she called.

Estelle came up behind her and put a hand on her arm. "Mr. O'Brian isn't here, Christine. He left with George."

"He did?" That was odd. "Why? Where did they go? When will he be back?"

Estelle guided her into the living room and down onto the sofa. "I'm afraid he's not coming back." Estelle pressed her lips together. "After we talked, he agreed that you should come with me."

"Come with you?"

"That's right. To my clinic." She sighed. "You need professional help, Christine. There's no better place to get it than at my clinic. I've booked a flight for us to Miami. It leaves in a couple of hours. As soon as George returns..."

She went on talking, while Christine stared at her in numb dismay. Alec had just left, without even saying goodbye? Why had he done that? She'd spoken to him on the phone and he hadn't mentioned anything like that. He'd been anxious to see her again. He'd been worried about her! Why would he just...leave?

She took a look around the room, fighting the feeling that something was very, very wrong. Maybe she should just do as Estelle said and go to her clinic. Look how twitchy she was now. She could hardly sit still!

But none of this made any sense. Alec wouldn't want her to go to Estelle's clinic! And he certainly wouldn't leave without saying goodbye! A rescue wasn't over until the rescuer said it was over—that's what he'd told her. "No," she said. "It's very sweet of you to come, Estelle, but I don't need to go to your clinic. I'm really quite fine. Besides, I have to go back to work tomorrow." She jumped to her feet, anxious to be out of this room and out of this house. "Listen, we weren't, uh, expecting company. I think we're all out of vegetables and I'm not sure about the bread situation. I'll just zip into town and pick up a few groceries. Why don't you just stay here and—"

She took a step toward the door and froze as a large, unfamiliar male figure stepped into the doorway, blocking her exit.

"I'm terribly sorry, Christine," Estelle said from behind. "But I'm afraid I really must insist."

The man took a step forward, his heavy, square face filled with menace. Christine gasped, her stomach curling with fear. Her thumb gave a violent twitch, but Christine didn't need that to tell her she might be in big, big trouble.

"IT'S ALL THAT Alec O'Brian's fault," Estelle complained.

She paced across the living room, took a look out the window, then returned her attention to Christine. "You shouldn't have gotten involved with him. If you hadn't, none of this would have been necessary."

Christine was huddled on the sofa, struggling to absorb everything. "Why on earth would you want to hurt me? I thought we were friends."

"I didn't have any choice." Estelle sighed heavily. "You have to understand that. I never wanted to hurt you. I just asked Karl to...frighten you a little, that's all."

"Frighten me? Why?"

"Compulsive chronic memory syndrome. I've spent years researching it." Her face narrowed to an intense expression. "I know it exists. But my funding is about to run out—and there won't be any more federal grants, since I have never been able to find someone who is suffering from it." She made a helpless gesture. "When you had that accident in the parking lot, and told me about your thumb, well, I decided to see if I could produce the same effect myself." She smiled briefly. "It was sort of a clinical test, and it worked out very nicely—with Karl's help, of course."

Christine looked at the big blond man still standing directly in front of the door, then focused back on Estelle. "Karl? That's who was...was after me?"

"He wasn't really after you! I just asked him to frighten you. He's suffering from an aggravated sort of violence displacement—I'm afraid he quite enjoyed doing it." She gave Karl a stern look. "He wasn't supposed to blow up your brother's cabin, though. He was just supposed to start a little fire—to frighten you. But he got carried away. We'll have to do some work on that, Karl."

"Estelle!"

"And then you disappeared!" Estelle accused. "You shouldn't have done that! You should have come straight to my clinic! When you told me that you were near Cremona I had Karl come out here to look for you. He couldn't ask too many questions—I didn't want him to attract any attention—but I had him watch the golf course. I was pretty sure you'd turn up there. You are compulsive in that respect." Her forehead furrowed. "Karl did think he'd spotted you there, but you left before he could make certain of it."

So that's why her thumb had twitched! Christine felt a surge of triumph. She wasn't crazy after all. Her spirits plummeted almost immediately. She might not be crazy, but she wasn't exactly safe, either.

"When I realized you were with Mr. O'Brian, I came immediately. I thought I could talk him into dropping his investigation." She sighed deeply. "I was wrong. And after talking with him for a few minutes, it was apparent that he'd figured the whole thing out. He's quite a clever man, isn't he?"

"He's wonderful," Christine whispered. Her heart thudded with alarm. "Where is he really, Estelle?"

"George is...disposing of him."

Christine could practically feel the blood drain out of her face. "Disposing of him?"

"George will make it look like an accident. He'll just drown in the river, that's all. He was totally unconscious when he left, so I don't expect that he'll feel a thing. And I doubt that his body will be found for some time."

"No," Christine murmured. "No." She started to

rise. "I don't believe any of this. You wouldn't do that. You..."

Karl's top lip curled. He took a step toward her. "I wouldn't make any sudden moves if I were you," Estelle advised. "Karl is very...jumpy. And he does enjoy hurting people—I'm afraid Mr. O'Brian found that out."

Christine sat back down. "You are serious, aren't you?"

"Yes, I am." Estelle's dark blue eyes were filled with anguish. "I didn't want to hurt him. If he just would have left it alone! But he wouldn't."

"And what about me?" Christine demanded. "If you think I'm going to go along with this, you're wrong! Or are you planning on disposing of me, too?"

"That won't be necessary." Estelle's narrow face was filled with determination. "After a few days in my clinic you'll forget all about this. And even if you told someone, no one would believe you. Compulsive chronic memory syndrome. They'll probably name it after you."

The room settled into silence, immediately broken by the sound of a car engine. "That's George," Estelle said. She opened her purse, pulled out a tube and dumped a syringe into her hand. "This could hurt for a moment, but then you'll feel literally nothing—and you'll be as docile as a lamb for the trip." She began walking toward Christine. "Actually, you should be glad—you won't have to worry about a thing for the next several months."

Christine took a deep breath, trying to clear her panicking brain. She had very little chance of getting out of this alive, but anything would be better than going with these people and being turned into a specimen for human research. And she wasn't going to let them get away with killing Alec—not without making some attempt to save him...or avenge him.

She put a hand into her pocket and closed her fingers around a golf ball. It wasn't much of a weapon, but it was better than nothing. "I'm really sorry, Estelle," she said as she sprang to her feet. "But I just don't feel like having a mythical syndrome named after me."

She drew back her arm like the professional she used to be and threw the golf ball as hard and fast as she could straight at Karl's forehead. Karl let out a yell as the missile smashed into his face. He took a few staggering steps backward, into the hall. Christine gave Estelle a violent shove facedown onto the sofa and yanked the syringe out of her hand, having some hazy notion of using it on Karl. She took a step toward him and froze.

Karl had regained his balance, but he wasn't moving toward her. Instead, he was clutching a nasty-looking gun, aimed directly at her. Christine heard the gun click, signifying its readiness to fire, then gasped in surprise as a man hurtled down the hall, tackling Karl to the floor.

The gun went off with a horrendous bang. Estelle started to rise, but Christine shoved her down again, holding her with one knee, and watched in total disbelief as the newcomer rose to his feet, the gun now in his possession. "Alec?"

He turned slowly to face her. "Hi, Chrissy. Are you okay?"

"Yes, but..." She gaped at him. He looked distinctly worse for wear. His entire face seemed to be swelling, one hand was clutching his side and his pupils were growing larger by the minute. "What happened to you, Alec? They told me they were...they were, uh, disposing of you."

Alec shrugged that off. "I suppose that was their intention." He raised a hand to massage the back of his head. "I must admit they gave it a good try."

"You're all wet."

"Yeah, well, George and I had a difference of opinion about who was going to be thrown in the river." He blinked thoughtfully. "I wonder if George can swim."

"Oh, Alec."

"I think I've knocked this guy out, too." He stared down at Karl for a moment, then stumbled across the room toward her and put an arm around her shoulders. "Are you okay?"

"Yes, but..."

"Good." He hugged her briefly, then focused on Estelle, his eyes narrowing. "How about if you go call the police while I have a few words with our master villain? I think it's safe to let her up now." His tone darkened. "She's not going anywhere."

Christine studied his expression. "You wouldn't...hurt her, would you?"

"Hurt her?" Alec's eyes widened. "Gee, Chrissy, she tried to make you think you were crazy, had her goons beat me up and was planning to have me killed." His eyebrows lowered. "Why in the world would I want to hurt her?"

"Alec!"

He grinned crookedly and patted her shoulder. "It's okay, honey. I just want to interview her."

"Interview her?"

"Uh-huh." He rubbed an eye, then bent to pick his notepad off the floor where it had fallen. "Every great rescue mission should get written up in the newspaper."

13

"WHEN YOU DIG for a story, you really dig for a story," Harper enthused.

"Uh-huh." Alec sat in the hospital bed and fingered the bandages on his left side. He'd always suspected having a cracked rib wouldn't be much fun. Unfortunately, he'd been right. His side ached like crazy. So did his head, where Estelle's goon had smashed his temple. The next time he rescued someone, he was going to pack a ton of painkillers.

Which reminded him of the rescue mission he'd just wrapped up. He turned his head slowly to check out the other people in the room. There was quite a crowd—people from work, a lot of relatives, some of the sports figures in town. However, there was one person who had yet to make an appearance. "Where's Chrissy?" he asked Harper.

Harper shrugged a pin-striped shoulder. "Chicago."

"Chicago?" Alec gave his head a slight shake, which was definitely the wrong thing to do just then. "What's she doing in Chicago?"

"HoleSum has some sort of promotion thing going

on there." Harper chuckled slightly. "HoleSum sure got some good publicity out of this—not to mention the *Centennial*. You and Christine are all over the news."

"Just a minute. Are you telling me that I rescued that woman, I got beat up for her, I almost went out of my mind with worry about her and she's off selling bean sprouts?"

Harper's big bushy eyebrows lowered. "I don't know if she's selling bean sprouts, but..."

The room circled around Alec, making him feel sick to his stomach. It wasn't the pain in his side that was doing it, he realized. It was the idea that Christine wasn't going to be part of his life anymore. Apparently that was how she saw their rescue ending—with her going off and leaving him behind.

"No," he said. He pushed away the covers. "No. We're involved, damn it."

"Lie down, O'Brian. You're not going anywhere. You—"

"Besides, I didn't say this rescue was over. She doesn't get to just leave!"

"Alec..."

"What's the matter with her, anyway?" Alec asked Harper. "I clearly told her that the knight and the damsel had to live happily ever after. It's a basic requirement of a rescue."

"You're not making a whole lot of sense." Harper put a big hand on Alec's shoulder. "And you shouldn't be moving around. You had one hell of a concussion when they brought you in last night. If you get up, you might pass out."

Alec swung himself out of the bed. "I am not going to pass out," he growled. "I am going to throw up. Then I am going to pass out. And after that, I'm going to find Christine. And this time I will see to it that she never, ever disobeys another rule."

"THANK YOU, Mr. Kleinghammer," Christine murmured. "I'll give it serious consideration."

She shook hands with the gray-haired, distinguished-looking president of HoleSum Foods and climbed into the taxi waiting to take her back to her hotel. The rain splattered against the window as they wended their way through the darkening Chicago streets. It seemed to have been raining ever since she got here, Christine grumbled to herself. Either that or her dejected mood made it appear that way.

She tried to shake off her depression as she paid the taxi driver and wandered into the hotel. There was no reason for her to be feeling this way. She had everything she wanted. Her mental health was no longer in question. Estelle and her henchmen were safely locked away. All the sponsors for the inner-city children's program were committed. HoleSum had offered to renew her contract for two more years.

So why was she miserable?

She entered the elevator and pressed the button for

her floor. Maybe she was just upset because of Estelle. They had been friends for a long time—at least Christine had thought they were friends. But obviously they hadn't been, not really. Estelle couldn't have cared too much about her. She'd been perfectly willing to sacrifice Christine for the sake of her work. That's all Estelle had really cared about—her work.

Christine stepped out of the elevator and fumbled through her purse for the card key to her room. The really depressing thought was that she wasn't sure she was any better than Estelle. She didn't have much in her life besides her work.

She pulled the key out of her purse, sighing. She didn't want it to be this way. She had no desire to spend another evening in a hotel room, all by herself, reading marketing reports. She wasn't interested in climbing into another airplane, flying to another city, making another public appearance. She didn't want to hock bean sprouts anymore. She wanted to be back in Marty's house, being protected by Alec.

Her rescue had ended two days ago, in a Calgary hospital. Alec's injuries hadn't been too serious, but the hospital had insisted on keeping him there. Christine had made a statement to the police, several to the press, and had spent the night in a hotel. Alec had been groggy when she'd stopped at the hospital to see him the next morning. His room had been filled with family and friends, and she hadn't been able to do more than whisper a thank-you in his ear, squeeze his hand and kiss his cheek.

She swallowed away the empty feeling in her heart. Perhaps leaving so abruptly hadn't been the right thing to do. Maybe if she'd stayed...

She gave her head a shake and slid the key into the slot. She couldn't have stayed in Calgary. She'd had the store opening to attend. Besides, there wasn't anything to stay for. The mission was over. She had her work, and Alec was probably busy falling into bed with some other woman.

She grimaced at the thought, put her hand on the doorknob and gave it a turn. As she did, her thumb gave one slight, small, involuntary twitch.

Christine yanked her hand away from the door as if it had been burned and frowned down at her thumb. "We're not starting that again, are we?"

Her thumb twitched again.

Christine tightened her lips, took a deep breath and swung open the door.

There was a man in her room. He was sprawled on the bed, apparently watching some sporting event on television. He was of medium height, with carelessly combed, sandy brown hair, and his good-looking face sported a sizable bruise on the right cheek. He wore a pair of faded blue jeans with a hole in the knee, a white T-shirt and a brown tweed jacket, and her heart pretty much stopped beating when she looked at him.

"Hi, Chrissy," he said.

Christine swallowed a couple of times and pushed the door closed behind her, keeping her gaze on him all the while. "Alec?"

"It's me, all right." He used the remote-control to turn off the television and carefully eased himself to his feet.

Christine couldn't stop staring at him. "What, uh...what are you doing here?"

"That's exactly what I was going to ask you." He strolled across the room toward her. "You haven't got the hang of this rescue business yet, have you?"

Christine was having trouble concentrating on his words. She was too busy fighting the desire to run across the room, throw her arms around him and beg him to stay here with her. "I haven't?"

"No." His dimple flashed with a quick smile. "When the rescuer is in the hospital, recovering from near-fatal injuries he received on the rescuee's behalf, she is not supposed to go sell a truckload of carrot juice. She is supposed to be weeping by his bedside and telling him he's wonderful."

"Near fatal?" Christine echoed. She took a step toward him, her gaze wandering over him, checking for injuries. Underneath the purple bruise on his right cheek his face did seem pale, and in spite of his light-hearted tone, the usual sparkle seemed to be missing from his eyes. "They told me you had a cracked rib and a concussion."

"The extent of my injuries is not the point. I was still hurt. I was in the hospital and you..." He aimed a finger at her. "You should have been there."

"I was there," Christine objected. "I talked to the doctor myself. He said you were going to be okay. There were reporters all over the place...dozens of people in your room...."

"So you just...left?"

"Well, yes, but..."

He stopped in front of her. "That's another rule you've broken. You weren't supposed to wander off without telling me. I thought you could remember that rule, considering we've been through it more than once."

Christine studied him with some concern. Perhaps that concussion had been more serious than she'd thought. "The rescue is over, Alec."

"No, it isn't. A rescue isn't over until the rescuer says it's over."

Christine smiled faintly. "I do remember that, but..."

He leaned a slumped shoulder against the wall beside her. "Well, if you're waiting for me to say it, you can forget it."

"What?"

"I don't want it to end." He bent his head to examine his fingernails. "Don't you know what happens during a rescue mission? The rescuer and the rescuee fall madly, passionately and hopelessly in love." He glanced up at her. "It happens in all the best rescues."

Christine's heart finally started beating again—with slow, smashing beats. "It does?"

"Yeah, it does." He sighed and shoved a hand through his hair in a gesture that was so familiar a lump formed in Christine's throat. "Then they ride off into the sunset and live happily ever after. Together."

Christine didn't say anything.

Alec drew in a breath and looked directly into her eyes. "You must care something about me, Chrissy. After all, we are involved. Or did we stop being involved between my getting bashed on the head and waking up in the hospital, and I missed it?"

Christine hesitated, then shook her head. "You didn't miss anything."

Alec let out a gusty sigh. "That's a relief." He straightened and took a final step toward her. "Listen, I know there are things about me you don't like. I'm lazy. I'm irresponsible. I'm unambitious. But some of those things can change. For example, I plan never again to mention a female athlete's knees in my column." He grinned fleetingly. "And as a matter of fact, after the fabulously insightful and extremely deep article I wrote about you, my boss is under the impression that I'll be doing the same thing at least once a week. Surprisingly enough, I'm looking forward to trying." He fingered the bruise on his cheekbone. "I just hope I don't have to get beat up all the time to accomplish it."

"I wouldn't think—"

"And one of the local radio stations has asked me to do a spot for them on a regular basis. That should be something of a challenge."

"I'm sure it would. Alec, you don't have to—"

"I've got good points, too," he continued. "I'm decent-enough looking—at least I was before some goon smashed up my face. I can be incredibly charming. And—" he made a wry grimace "—as cliché as it sounds, I am hopelessly and madly and passionately in love with you." His gaze met hers, both the blue and green parts filled with sincerity. "Plus I did save you. That should count for something."

Christine's purse slipped from her fingers onto the floor.

"You're not perfect yourself, you know. You're far too serious—at least, you are without me around. You don't have any fun. I'm great at fun. You work too hard. I can make sure you don't do that." He raised a hand to stroke a finger down her cheek. "We'd make a great combination. I could rescue you from yourself and you could rescue me from myself. We could spend our lives together, rescuing each other."

Christine didn't hesitate. She threw her arms around him and pulled his head down to hers. "It sounds perfect."

"AND I'LL SPEAK to the HoleSum people about letting me do the charity work I like without having to do all the 'hocking bean sprouts' part," Christine concluded. She patted Alec's bare chest, rested her head on it and yawned. "There would be a lot less travel, so I'll be around to make sure you're not eating too much junk food."

"We'll, uh, work out a compromise," Alec mumbled. "Marriages always involve a lot of compromise." He hesitated. "You do understand that we're talking about marriage, don't you?"

"Well, you haven't exactly asked, but..."

"I would have if you hadn't started ripping off my clothes."

Christine flushed. "I didn't..."

A chuckle rumbled through his chest. "Yeah, you did. Will you marry me?"

Christine closed her eyes. "Yes."

"Yes?" He raised her chin and angled his head, frowning. "You're not supposed to just say yes. You're supposed to tell me that you are hopelessly in love with me—or words to that effect." He paused. "Assuming that's how you feel, of course."

Christine rolled onto him and looked down into his battered but still incredibly good-looking face. The green in his eyes sparkled at her, but the blue showed a hint of uncertainty. "You're wonderful," she told him. "You're brilliant and marvelous, and I am madly and passionately and hopelessly in love with you."

His grin told her that was exactly what he wanted to hear. "Good thing," he grumbled. "There are severe penalties for not being in love with me." He eased her head back down onto his shoulder. "Now here's the first rule of marriage. You have to tell me those words several times a day. The wife has to tell her husband he's brilliant, wonderful and that she's hopelessly in love with him at least five times a day."

Christine didn't think she'd have much problem with that. "Okay," she murmured. She closed her eyes and was drifting off to sleep when she realized what he'd said. "Rules?" Her eyes popped open. "Did you mention something about...rules?"

"That's right." Alec grinned cheerfully. "There are rules for a marriage, too. That was the first rule. The second rule is that you have to do all the cooking. The third is no healthy food. And the fourth..."

Christine groaned and began pummeling him with a pillow.

Spoil yourself next month
with these four novels from

Temptation ®

SEDUCED BY A STRANGER by Morgan Hayes

P.I. Mack Carlino had finally found Teddy Logan. Now he was
supposed to hand her over to her irate fiancé. Unfortunately,
Mack couldn't keep his hands off her. Their lovemaking was
explosive...and soon Mack had a problem—how to tell his client
that his runaway fiancée had found a replacement...

THE RETURN OF DANIEL'S FATHER by Janice Kaiser

Ethan Mills was back to clear his name and claim his only son,
Daniel. But Kate Rawley had raised her nephew since her sister
died in childbirth. Now Ethan wanted time with Daniel—and her.
She couldn't deny her attraction to Ethan...but when it came to
Daniel's future, a tug of love could only become a tug of war...

MICHAEL: THE DEFENDER by JoAnn Ross

New Orleans Lovers

Someone wanted to hurt beautiful movie star Lorelei
Longstreet—so private detective Michael O'Malley had been
hired to guard her, day and night. For Lorelei, being with
Michael brought back memories of their love affair years ago.
Michael might protect her from danger, but who would protect
Lorelei from him?

BOARDROOM BABY by Molly Liholm

When Robert Devlin found out that his sexy co-worker, Kate
Ross, had become pregnant via a clinic, he had a dreadful
suspicion that he was the baby's father. This wasn't the way he'd
planned to meet the mother of his children! But soon Devlin
didn't care if his plans had changed—so long as they all involved
him, Kate and *their* baby!

On sale from 1st June 1998

4 FREE

books and a surprise gift!

We would like to take this opportunity to thank you for reading this Mills & Boon® book by offering you the chance to take FOUR more specially selected titles from the Temptation® series absolutely FREE! We're also making this offer to introduce you to the benefits of the Reader Service™—

- ★ FREE home delivery
- ★ FREE gifts and competitions
- ★ FREE monthly newsletter
- ★ Books available before they're in the shops
- ★ Exclusive Reader Service discounts

Accepting these FREE books and gift places you under no obligation to buy, you may cancel at any time, even after receiving your free shipment. Simply complete your details below and return the entire page to the address below. *You don't even need a stamp!*

YES! Please send me 4 free Temptation books and a surprise gift. I understand that unless you hear from me, I will receive 4 superb new titles every month for just £2.30 each, postage and packing free. I am under no obligation to purchase any books and may cancel my subscription at any time. The free books and gift will be mine to keep in any case.

T8XE

Ms/Mrs/Miss/Mr..................................Initials ....
BLOCK CAPITALS PLEASE

Surname ....

Address ....

....

....Postcode..................................

Send this whole page to:
THE READER SERVICE, FREEPOST, CROYDON, CR9 3WZ
(Eire readers please send coupon to: P.O. BOX 4546, DUBLIN 24.)

This month's
irresistible novels from

OUT OF CONTROL by Candace Schuler
Blaze

Andrea Wagner had been without a man for eight years—but she didn't want one unless she could be in control—on and off the job. Then Jim Nicolosi started working for her. He had a slow, seductive touch, the body of an adonis... He wanted her in his arms, out of control. *And she wanted to be there.*

SHAYNE: THE PRETENDER by JoAnn Ross
New Orleans Lovers

His superiors were convinced Bliss Fortune was part of an international jewel-smuggling ring, but undercover operative Shayne O'Malley was having other ideas. He wondered if this trusting, passionate woman might be innocent. But that meant someone was setting her up...

THE BRIDE RODE WEST by Kristine Rolofson
Brides on the Run

On her wedding day, Emilie Grayson had caught her fiancé in a torrid embrace. So she headed west as fast as she could and ended up as a housekeeper for rancher Matt Thomson and his three daughters. The fact she found him irresistibly attractive had nothing to do with her staying on... *Absolutely nothing!*

RESCUING CHRISTINE by Alyssa Dean

Reporter Alec O'Brian didn't believe Christine McKinley's life was in danger—until his story led to another 'accident'. It was up to him to find out who wanted to hurt her—and why. But when he'd finished rescuing Christine, would she have any more use for a hero?